No, I can’t make round rotis

No, I can't make round rotis

Stories of guts and grace

RICHA DHAWAN

Prestige Books International

New Delhi

Published by
Prestige Books International
New Delhi 110 060
prestigebooks@gmail.com
Phones: +91 9818755529; +919810323134

Associate Office
11b, Broomwood Road
London SW11 6HU, U.K.

Associate Office
P.O. Box 2250
Sydney 2001, Australia

The characters and events portrayed in this book are fictitious. Any similarity to real persons, alive or dead, is co-incidental and not intended by the author.

ISBN 978-81-947512-1-2
Printed in India

Contents

Preface

This book is my first attempt at fiction and stems from my experiences as a girl, woman, mother and a prolific traveler.

The 13 stories in this collection represent an amalgamation of experiences. 'Being woman' is still not easy, even in 2020.

Through *No, I can't make round rotis*, my innermost voice has been able to travel through the intricacies of language and vocabulary in story forms that I hope you will find interesting.

Even though the stories are fictitious, many of you will be able to relate to them. Why? Because all of these are inspired by real events and experiences of a generation of women in urban India.

On a lighter note, to date, I cannot make round rotis.

Why I write

Why do I write? It is indeed a vexing question—not easy to answer. The desire to express oneself and the urge to reveal the 'world within' has universal connotations. This, I believe, is stronger in the case of women who try to express their feelings through the medium of art.

'Every life is a story worth telling!' Self-narrative does not only ask the question 'Who am I'; it also asks and answers the query, 'How did I become what I am'? The act of writing for me—and for many others like me—assumes importance because it is through writing that the self and life take a specific dimension and image.

The pandemic coronavirus has threatened our very existence. We are living in a critical time—a sword of Damocles hanging over our heads—a situation in which anything disastrous could happen to us. It is time we go back to our roots and evaluate life in all its totality.

Writing can be deeply therapeutic. It can be a way to express our fears, hopes and joys. It can help us make sense of the world and our place in it. Most of the people don't know the purpose of their lives; otherwise they will be able to choose a path that will help them discover the ability to fulfil that purpose with the glory that it deserves.

I have been born and brought up in India—a country of immense possibilities. I had a long sojourn in Sydney, where I studied further and raised my family. Australia's vast spaces and landscape broadened my vision of life—it was a dream to have come to this exotic country. And currently I am in Singapore—a place that has given me balance and stability—very characteristic of this country. Amazingly, it is a city, island, and country—all in one. It is a place of rich cultural diversity that I find highly conducive to the catering of my creative urge.

Many of my friends ask me which of the three countries moulded me the most—my answer is India: I carry Delhi deep inside me because it is the city where I was born, grew up, was formed, and lived those experiences of childhood and youth that shaped my personality and forged my calling.

India is a country you can never leave behind. It's an amazing place though it is disturbing to see how, despite the massive resurgence, the disparate issues and the problems it is facing could not be pulled together. We wonder how and why has the enormous inequality and glaring socio-economic disparity become the mainstay of our lives?

I have been able to address, however inadequately, my larger concerns that engage my compassion and sense of justice. What we need to learn as a community is how much connected we are, how compassionate and empathetic we are? And do we care for animals and for the environment?

I've been writing my stories from the perspective of a young woman. These stories are about how millennial women live. What they think about, talk about, all circling one word: choice. Indeed, we have won the freedom to determine the course of our lives. How do we know we are making the right choice? We have the chance to interrogate both—the lives that we once led and consider the ones that we hope to lead.

Woman today has appeared in a new avatar: she is no more a 'damsel in distress'. She ceases to be an object of pleasure. No one ever has the right to demand access to others' bodies, and you never owe anyone access to your body—regardless of how you look, what skin colour you have, what clothing you wear. It is your business, none of others.

People ask me how I transitioned from being a doctor to being a writer. The reason: I had a passion, a yearning. I realised that there was an author trapped inside me who wanted to break free. Writing is a cognitive activity: we don't know what we are going to write until we actually do. Today technology has come in but the soul is lost. The writer is obliged to unravel the deep, enigmatic mysteries of life in our search for the elusive truth.

By all means, India is linguistically and culturally diverse. Given its rich cultural history coupled with the new challenges and aspirations of its peoples, there are myriad stories to be told. And some of these stories—dear readers—I wish to share with you today. I humbly hope these will be able to resonate with you all.

Richa Dhawan

Nimbu Paani

Reena was the eldest of the four siblings, with two younger sisters and a younger thirteen-year-old brother. She was the ideal Indian daughter who was raised with immense love and affection. She belonged to a family that valued their alpha males, just like primates do.

Consequently, Reena became a quaint and domesticated goddess who had the skills to be the world's greatest homemaker, and she did become one. She had just finished the final exams of her bachelor's degree in Hindi, through 'distance-learning' from University of Delhi. She was the legitimate *wife-material* and was all set to get married now. Her paternal uncle came up with a marriage proposal, recommending his friend's son, Vikas, a small-time businessman based in Sydney, Australia.

Reena and Vikas met at Reena's house in the presence of both the families. Reena was too shy to talk to anyone. But she cooked an elaborate feast, a common practice in India on such a rendezvous. Reena's welcome drink *Nimbu Paani,* a lemonade, was the first thing about Reena that Vikas and his entire family fell in love with—love at first sip. It was an exotic drink. It had rose petals, mint leaves and just the right proportions of few of the hundred spices from Reena's mythical pantry. It looked like Vikas and his family wanted Reena's Nimbu Paani to come to their family and become their legacy. Reena and Vikas got married and moved to Sydney a month later.

Vikas ran an Indian clothing store in a Sydney suburb called Harris Park. It was a rented shop and was performing moderately. There were some high sales periods each year, especially around Diwali time. Vikas had rented a two-bedroom apartment in Harris Park as it was close to his store.

It looked like Reena had entered a pact of becoming *the perfect wife.* Every day, after Vikas left for work, Reena would get busy in housekeeping, laundry, ironing, and cooking. She made fresh lunch for Vikas, along with tea; and brought it daily to the store, at precisely 1 p.m. She considered her life peachy, enjoying the marital bliss, with her new alpha male. Lucky for Reena, this one was mellow and appeared to care about her. She felt triumphant on scoring a considerate husband.

Weeks and months went by. Reena decided that she wanted to change the curtains in the living room from chocolate brown colour to bright sunlight yellow. She had a feeling this would give the room much-needed brightness and life. She decided to make her curtains. So, after handing over the lunch-box to Vikas one day, Reena decided to take the train and go to *Spotlight*, a giant fabric raw material store, to buy curtain-making material. She went to Harris Park train station to board the Sydney public transport train.

It was a chilly Sydney in May afternoon. The people at the station were scarce. There was just a tradie and Reena, ready to board the train at Platform 1, towards the city. Suddenly, Reena saw a woman, who appeared to be in her late twenties, sitting on a bench behind the pillar. She seemed to be asleep. Reena tried to look closely and saw a bruise on the lady's forehead. The train was still thirteen minutes away, and curiously she decided to check on her.

As Reena got a few steps closer, she saw the woman was dressed elegantly. She wore a beautiful coat which looked royal and expensive. Her makeup was flawless, and she had let her beautiful long black hair down. Her black quilted handbag with shiny stitches made Reena feel a bit intimidated because she had seen the same bag on the cover of a magazine, a couple of days ago. Observing with intent, Reena was in awe of the lady's beautiful dark brown ankle-length boots with golden zippers. But her most striking feature was her blood-red lipstick. Reena always wondered how people gathered the courage to wear something so bold. In Reena's head, wearing red lipstick was equivalent to wearing a bikini; where both the actions required a lot of confidence and guts.

Reena said to herself—*what if this woman is in some kind of crisis?* She decided to help and said to the woman, 'the train is coming soon'.

The woman opened her eyes very slowly; looked at Reena and said, 'I know. I am just taking a nap.'

Reena got somewhat suspicious because the woman's eyes were a bit red—the kind of redness that comes after hours of crying. Reena said, 'Are you alright? You've got a bruise on your forehead.'

She replied hesitatingly, 'I am fine . . . thanks.' She then tried to stand but collapsed back on the bench.

She said to Reena and explained, 'I think I've been sitting here for too long. My legs are a bit numb.'

She then extended her right hand towards Reena and said, 'Care to help?'

Reena smiled and gladly went forward and helped the woman get up and walk.

'I am Nitya, by the way. Thanks a lot.'

'No problem. I am Reena. But how did you get hurt on your forehead?'

'Oh! I just hit my head against the pole while entering the station. It's nothing.'

'Where are you headed, Ms Nitya'?

'I am just getting off at the next stop.'

'I've heard that there's a big shopping centre at the next stop. Would it be too much to ask if I wanted to stick around for a while? I've had a rough day, and I have a feeling that spending time with a friendly stranger like you might help. You seem nice.'

Reena felt awkward, 'But I need to buy fabric for my new curtains.'

'That's not a problem. I would love to help you. Honestly, I could use a little distraction right now from my life. And we could have something to eat as well. My treat. What do you say, Reena?'

Reena's mind went off at a tangent, and she had anxiety showing all over her face. She wasn't sure if she wanted to. Nitya was a stranger, after all. It was baffling.

Nitya pleaded, 'Look, I understand this is awkward, and you may be thinking about me as an intruder. I urge you to please trust me. I am not a burglar . . . just a woman who wants to make friends with you. I promise. I won't harm you in any way.'

Reena was taken aback by Nitya's insistence, her desperation. She looked distressed, and it was Reena's obligation as a human being to help her out.

'Okay. Let's go. The train is here,' Reena said.

They both got off at the next stop—Parramatta. Reena and Nitya purchased everything Reena needed for her new curtains from Spotlight. Then, they sat down at a café and started talking over sandwiches and coffee.

'So Reena, did you just move to Australia?'

'Three months ago. My husband has an Indian clothing store in Harris Park. In fact, that's where we live.'

'And what do you do? I mean professionally!'

'I love up-keeping my house. Cleaning, laundry, ironing, groceries, and cooking. All that is my job.'

'But you don't get paid for all that.'

'Not in money. But I am a pillar of my house. Today, my husband needs me, and in the future, my kids will need me too.'

Nitya laughed out loud.

'You don't have to mock me. I love being a housewife. And besides, my husband is great. He takes good care of me, and he respects me.'

Nitya immediately regretted her laughter. 'I am sorry, Reena. It was inappropriate. I guess I am not as lucky as you in finding men.' And Nitya started crying.

Reena tried to comfort her by holding her hand.

'Reena, I was wondering if you would want to have coffee with me again?'

'I'd love to,' said Reena as she waved goodbye.

Reena returned home and couldn't stop thinking about a million possible stories associated with Nitya's strange and secretive life. She finished the curtains and also sewed tablecloths, cushion covers and pillowcases. Vikas couldn't stop appreciating Reena's craft and sewing skills.

Vikas loved Reena's qualities of head and heart. He said, 'I am so grateful I found you, Reena. You are amazing.' Reena felt even more for Nitya after that. She kept thinking about the bruise on her forehead day after day.

After four days, Reena got a text from Nitya asking her to meet in about thirty minutes. She had just finished making her epic Nimbu Paani and decided to give it to Nitya. So, she packed some in a bottle and rushed to the same café at Parramatta. Nitya was waiting for Reena seated at a table.

'I've got something for you, Nitya. Taste my *Nimbu Paani*.'

Nitya gladly had a sip and was amazed, 'Reena, aren't you a *Nimbu Paani* wizard? When life gives you lemons, make Reena's *Nimbu Paan*i!'

They talked for a couple of hours. Nitya went down the memory lane, mostly talking about her childhood roaming around from city to city in India. That is because she was the daughter of an Army officer. She had all the freedom she wanted. She studied Financial Management and was now working as a consultant at a big firm in the city. She even told Reena that she lost her virginity at the age of seventeen with her first boyfriend. She had had three boyfriends before the fourth one, to whom she got married before coming to Sydney, six years ago.

'I love Sydney. But I miss my friends and family. I haven't had the time to make any friends since I came here. Work has been crazy, and I have been under the pump. I have a nice cosy house and nice cars, but I am lonely.' Nitya finished with a long face.

Reena felt sorry for her. 'Would you like to come to my house for dinner? Tomorrow night? It is Saturday, and maybe, you could bring your husband too.'

'I am busy tomorrow.'

'Some other day! Just pick one, Nitya.'

'I will let you know. Could I come during the day? Lunchtime?'

'Cool.'

'I want to take this leftover *Nimbu Paani* to my house to drink with my late-night hunger pangs tonight.'

Reena laughed. 'Sure.'

Reena again met Nitya over a cup of coffee the following Tuesday. Their friendship had passed the embryonic stage and was blooming now.

Nitya took Reena's hand and asked her, 'Reena, I know you love managing the house, and you do it so beautifully. But what if Vikas hadn't been so supportive? Would you still be happy to do it for him?'

'I would still do it because that's all I know.'

'You might not know how great a person you are, my friend. Vikas is so fortunate to have you.'

'Nitya, I am thankful to God for Vikas too. Moreover, I am not as great as you imagine. I don't know why you haven't been able to read me yet. I am scared to fall in the trap.'

'What do you mean?'

Reena sighed and began, 'My cousin, Khushboo, got married at twenty-two to a thirty-four years old man in Amritsar last year. She was great at managing the house too, but she wanted to be a teacher. She kept fighting for it, and he didn't let her. He maltreated her, called her names, abused her and beat her up until one day she decided to divorce him. But Khushboo's parents refused to let her back in their house if she opted for divorce. So, she had no choice. She wanted to end her life, but she got pregnant. Now, she is stuck with him for life. So, I decided to make myself happy in doing what I am expected to do. A woman's job!'

Nitya was shocked and her mouth wide open. 'What the hell? You are insane. That's so sad and so gross. Why don't you girls retaliate? Why are you so dependent on husbands or parents? It is disconcerting. Own up your life brazenly. Goddammit! You need to think about having some experience beyond the house. Honey, when you can be the exception, why be the rule?' Nitya couldn't get her head around the fact that Reena was, in fact, proud to sacrifice her desires and pose as a paragon of virtue.

'Easy tiger! And look who's talking? You are beginning to sound like a condescending movie star. Someone who doesn't know what's going outside her kingdom. Whereas you are a hypocrite. A person who needs to cover up a bruise with a fall before covering it up with a bandage. A person who can't even ask her husband to come over to her friend's place for dinner. You have the power, and regardless, you are miserable and helpless. I pity you even more than I do Khushboo. You need to own up your life first.' Nitya had provoked Reena.

They dispersed bitterly and didn't talk for the next few days. Then Nitya sent Reena a text—*Sorry for my outrage and misbehaviour. It was totally out of line. I am ashamed of myself. I don't want you to think that I am aloof. Give me another chance. If you still want to be friends with me, I am eager to see you. Would you please make your-out-of-the world nimbu paani for me? I would love to have it sitting next to the new curtains, again, made by you. Would you please forgive me for being ridiculous?*

Reena smiled for a couple of minutes and then invited Nitya over for lunch the next day at her house. Reena had grand plans for lunch. She had started preparing at 7 am and was making kebabs and biryani along with her signature *raita (yoghurt)*. Nitya had once disclosed how much she loved biryani. Reena also cooked saffron *kheer* for the dessert and lastly, *Nimbu Paani*.

Vikas helped Reena in the chopping and cutting before leaving for work. 'I am glad I married you, Vikas,' said Reena with gratitude. She considered herself fortunate to have found a husband who was better than everyone else's. Reena pitied Nitya and Khushboo and all other women in such situations more than ever. However, initially, she just had sympathy towards Nitya, but now, she felt she had found a great friend in her.

Reena ran to Vikas' store and dropped off the lunch-box and a bottle of *nimbu paani* plus a tea flask in a jiffy and returned home to receive Nitya. She was excited and jittery and kept hoping that Nitya likes her cooking and that her house doesn't seem too small to the fancy Nitya. And soon she opened the door in response to the bell.

Reena greeted Nitya with a big smile who, in turn, hugged Reena and started crying.

'I am so sorry, Reena. I can see how smart you are. I was a fool to be so brutal to you. I don't want to lose you, sweetheart.'

Reena wiped off her tears and hugged her back until she stopped crying. They both smiled, and Reena showed Nitya the couch. She then offered her the *nimbu paani,* and it brought a big smile on Nitya's face.

They got talking. Nitya was amazed by Reena's craft. She couldn't believe her eyes when she saw the curtains Reena had stitched off the raw material they bought together. 'Reena, you are an artist. Your work is outstanding.'

They moved to the dining table, and Nitya was full of praise for Reena's food. She loved the flavours of the biryani and the tenderness of the kebabs.

Reena then gathered a lot of courage and asked, 'Do you think you trust me enough now to spill your secrets?'

Nitya stared at her for a while and said, 'I trust you to keep the secrets, but I am not sure if you will be able to deal with the grief that comes with them. You are a delicate flower, and I don't want to crush you with my big disclosure.'

Reena was agitated. 'Don't you worry about crushing me. I am stronger than I look. Moreover, I want to be a part of your life. Otherwise, what's the point of this superficial friendship? I am sure this is not just about my *Nimbu Paani*. Is it, Nitya?'

Nitya was hesitant. She shook her head in refusal.

Reena insisted, 'I am not going to judge you. I can't. I admire you, but I can't see you suffer in silence. Share with me. I can be your listening friend.'

Nitya said in a harsh voice, 'I have done something terrible.'

Reena's eyes became wide, but she was confident of being helpful and also extremely persistent. 'Please tell me. I insist. I don't care what you did. I promise to be on your side.'

Nitya took a deep sigh and said, 'I killed my husband, Reena!'

Reena was aghast. Her jaw dropped in shock, and she felt like she was about to collapse. She got scared and anxious. She had sweat on her forehead, and her hands started to get clammy.

Nitya had tears rolling down her cheeks. She began to sob loudly. She then caught her breath and started with her life story. Nitya was 28 years old when she met him. His fourth boyfriend, her dead husband, Tarun, was in the Indian army. Just like her father. She met him at a party at the army club, and he wooed her with his charm, six years ago, in Delhi. They went on a couple of dates, and it felt like true love. After five months of dating, he proposed marriage to Nitya, and she agreed. Her father was the happiest of all.

After a year of marriage, Nitya wanted to get pregnant, but since she was booming in her job and had a bright future to look forward to, Tarun talked her out of it. Then out of the blue, she got a job offer in Australia, which she was going to decline because of Tarun. Plus, she was disinclined to leave her father behind. But the job offer was so lucrative that she didn't have enough points to argue with herself. Tarun had often admired Australia as an ideal country for living. In the eye of his imagination, he had formed a fantabulous image of Australia—a country that has a fascinating Sydney harbour, crowned by the scenic Opera House. But, unlike the gender norms, Nitya had a job there, and Tarun was going to have to start from scratch. It was a crucial decision. Nitya passionately convinced Tarun to quit the army and move to Australia with her.

The benefits of Nitya's new job were extensive. A large pay-cheque, a prime location house with paid rent and a car. In fact, they didn't even need Tarun to work moneywise. In the hope of a new delightful life, they came to Sydney.

Tarun and Nitya started their life in Sydney in positivity. He was very supportive during the first few months of the move. Tarun had learned a lot from his short-lived army life and now was his chance to put it all to test. He took his time to pick the career of his choice and ended up where his heart was—opening a small and cosy cafe, at a hot and happening street, spending a hefty sum of dollars and putting in all the discipline and hard work. He did everything to make it work for a good long year. And Nitya knew how passionate and desperate and even optimistic Tarun was. But, alas, unfortunately, it turned out to be a failure and all the money Nitya had saved was gone with it. It was disappointing for Nitya, but extremely traumatic for Tarun. He felt like a failure.

And that's when the dark days began. Tarun had no control over himself. Nitya said to Reena, 'I was working my ass off, and he never lifted a finger to find any job or to do any housework for that matter. I let him overcome his PTSD. But I had a threshold. He wasn't incompetent; he was just unwilling and had gotten used to taking advantage of me. I was earning and saving well. But that wasn't enough for him. And one night, during our usual screaming at each other session, he said something that was long buried in his heart—*I had everything back in India. I gave up my life because of you. I hate you.'*

Amongst all the havoc, Nitya was still desperate to have a child, though Tarun was always miles away from the idea. After months of begging and getting refused, desperate Nitya took a significant step. She stopped taking her contraceptive pills without Tarun's knowledge.

And finally, last month, while Nitya was at work, she got the good news. 'I am pregnant', she said to Tarun as soon as she entered the living room, where he was lying on the couch.

He looked at her with utter shock and yelled, 'How the hell did this happen? We must get an abortion. This can't be happening. How will you continue to work? What will happen to the cash-flow?'

'How about I continue to work, and you can babysit for a while? I can work till the end of my pregnancy and then return to work after six weeks of delivery. Many single mothers do it alone. I'm lucky I have you.' Nitya said to Tarun with eyes full of tears of hope.

'I am already living in hell. I want to set up another cafe. I can't do it with a baby,' Tarun seemed pretty upset.

'But you can still set up your café. Just give the baby a few months initially. I will keep working, so you have enough money to set up after.' Nitya tried to calm him down.

Tarun growled like an angry tiger, 'I'm not some god-damn woman who will change diapers while my wife works. I'm a man. An ex-army man!'

Tarun's reaction was quite evident, for back home, he had grown up in a patriarchal set up which advocated a stereotypical atmosphere with men at work and women at hearth. He disdained the idea of being domesticated. Had Tarun and Nitya's story been the other way around, things would have been easily acceptable. Unfortunately! But in any scenario, either of the two must compromise for the sake of the baby. Willingly or not. Most women do it all over the world. Tarun felt emasculated.

Nitya ran upstairs to her bedroom, crying. She left the door unlocked with lurking impossible hope that he might come in and miraculously apologize. He went inside the bedroom and made her sit on the bed while she was sobbing inconsolably. He put his fingers into her hair and BAM. He pulled Nitya's hair back and slapped her on her cheek; her head hit on the edge of the bed. 'And that is how I got that bruise on my forehead.'

He then said, 'I told you, no baby. You are killing my dreams here. Your attempt to coerce me like this will not succeed.'

Tarun forced Nitya to the stairs, and said, 'My parents always said not to marry a woman who can't even make round *rotis*. I can see the logic behind that now. It means you are not willing to try to go the extra mile. Similarly, you won't do anything extra to be a good wife or a good mother either. So, you are playing tricks with me for selfish ends, making me do petty jobs for you. Forget it! You have to get rid of the baby. Willingly, or not?'

And just as he was trying to push her down the stairs, Nitya grabbed him from behind, and she pushed him instead. Tarun fell down the stairs head-on, hitting his head on every single stair on the way, as Nitya watched him with anguish but not a single moment of remorse. She didn't go downstairs to check if he was alive or dead. She just stood at the top of the staircase, frozen in horror. Her mind kept imagining the possibility of what could have happened if Tarun had succeeded in pushing *her*. She wanted her freedom. Her justice! He died after ten more minutes of profuse bleeding.

Nitya was on edge. She went next to his body only when she was sure he had stopped struggling. She quickly thought of a solution to clear herself out of the picture and called the police. She informed them that she had come home early from work to surprise her husband about her pregnancy. He got so excited that he ran downstairs to call their family back in India. That's when he slipped while rushing and bled to his death. They just believed Nitya.

The police examined everything and left the house late at night. An ambulance left with Tarun's body. It was all over, but Nitya couldn't breathe. Half of her body felt guilty, and the rest half felt justified. She was so distressed that she spent the night sitting on the couch in front of the TV. She dozed off on the couch and was woken up with the theme song of the *Morning show* at 7 am. She took a shower and dressed up boldly to hide the emotions running inside her. She needed armour to hide herself in to avoid the world looking at her guilt through her body. She wanted to soak in the truth in her pregnant body of a killer woman, searching for the happiness of becoming a mother, that she desired and that she deserved. She told herself that she did what had to be done, but her conscience kept pulling her down. She hid that conscience up with fancy clothing and make-up. She then started walking on the street, blindly and crossed a train station and got on board destined to nowhere. As a big crowd of university goers made her feel claustrophobic, she got off at the next random station to get a breather. She closed her eyes for a few minutes. 'That's where you found me, Reena.'

Reena was speechless. She knew that Nitya was extremely lucky for not having been convicted. She was full of tears after listening to Nitya's heart-breaking story. She was perplexed and swallowed her urge to say that she was terrified as well. She didn't want to be gullible to her parents' teachings of ethics and virtues in life. Contrarily, she tried to be mindful and do what she thought was rational and fair. She knew now that it wasn't fair for any of the species always to have an alpha male.

'You never have to repeat that to anyone. Promise me, Nitya, that you will never reveal this to anyone. I don't know if you should have done it. But I know that if there were absolutely anything else you could have, you would. Now stop cursing yourself. You are having a baby, and I will take care of you.'

Nitya nodded. She could finally breathe. When Reena offered to be her confidant, her legs were shaking with apprehension to trust her enough. Reena could have easily called Nitya a murderer. She could have expanded the horizon of Nitya's guilt. She could have even talked Nitya into confessing. Or worse, Reena could have secretly gone to the police.

But on the other hand, Reena rescued Nitya from living hell. She reassured her that she wasn't going to be alone. They both cried and hugged each other for a long time.

'Now, would you like some more of that *nimbu-paani*?' Reena asked Nitya to show her that they were going to be friends regardless. Nitya, with an ear to ear smile, responded, 'Of course my friend. It is my favourite drink.'

After Nitya left that day, Reena couldn't stop fiddling. Her deep-rooted doctrine of the alpha male notions was now being questioned at the fundamental level. Her brain was at war with her heart. *Why does a male have to be alpha? Why does being a man mean being in power? In fact, why does being a home-maker mean not being in control? Why don't men respect women's choices? Why did Tarun or any other man force his wife to abandon motherhood and keep working when he was simply expected to look after his baby. And why did her husband force Khushboo to be a mother when she wanted to be a teacher? To hell with this prejudice. To hell with this misogyny.,*

After a few days, Reena knew what she wanted to do. She was now inclined to pursue something. When she got married, she wanted Vikas to rise and shine. But now, she wanted to have something of her credibility. She knew Vikas was a caring husband, but he was still a man. So, she tried to play it right with him. But at the same time, she was freaking out.

Finally, one day after dinner, Reena made *Nimbu Paani* for Vikas and mustered courage and went up to him. After he took a sip and gave her a smile out of appreciation for the delicacy, in a voice full of confidence she proposed to him, 'Vikas, I want to take over your store. I know you are doing it only because you can't just give it up. But I will do it because it is what I want to do. I want you to find a job elsewhere. Somewhere where you are as passionate as I would be at your store.'

Vikas was taken aback. But he knew that Reena was right. He said, 'I always said that I am proud of you. I didn't know I would be so much more grateful one day. Thanks for everything, my love. You are my life. Yes, I want nothing more in life than to give up this shop and open a taxation office. Only, I never had the freedom or courage. But if you take over the shop, I can do it, sweetheart. All because of you.'

Reena was ecstatic. She said, 'And I can be myself all because of you.' It seldom happens when two people who are meant to be together, get to be.

Reena joined the store, and it took long strides. She organized it perfectly with her exceptional skills. She juxtaposed all the clothes in a way that they should have always been. She was not just a pleasant face to greet the customers but became the real strength of the store, the push that the store needed. She didn't forget her first love: *Nimbu Paani*. And she offered her *Nimbu Paani* at the store to all customers as a welcome gesture. It was evident by now that a lot could happen over a glass of *Nimbu paani*.

One afternoon, when Reena was working at the store, Nitya walked in with a pregnant belly of twenty weeks, and Reena smiled and ran off to her.

'I can't wait to hear it, Nitya. Tell me', said Reena holding *Nimbu Paani* she was about to offer Nitya.

Nitya extended her arm to take it, but Reena shook her head in dismissal and said, 'Only after you share the big news. Tell me what the sonographer said.'

Nitya smiled and came close to Reena and whispered in her ear, 'It's a girl. I feel so happy.'

And as Reena handed over *Nimbu Paani* to Nitya, they both smiled. Nitya took a sip and said, 'It's magical.'

Follow me on Instagram

As the day ended and the moon rose, it became difficult for Maya to endure the hopeless life she had been leading. The world had led her to believe she was good for nothing and her life had no worth. So, she decided to quit and end it all. But before doing so, she wanted to take a stroll in the inner circle of Connaught Place, the elite business hub of New Delhi.

She had done this with her father umpteen times as a child. Connaught Place had a plethora of branded stores long before shopping malls had arrived in Delhi. Maya and her father disliked shopping. They would bond over the Hot Chocolate Fudge at *Nirula's*—the fast-food restaurant. Then, they would just stroll around the circular path and chat while waiting for Maya's mother to finish shopping. Maya's mother often bought stuff only to exchange it sooner or later, which both father and daughter found exasperating. This continued as a Connaught Place father-daughter-customary-activity every weekend until her father died in a car crash nine years ago. Maya missed him more than ever.

She started wandering, waiting either to get lost in the maze of life or else kill herself to embrace perennial refuge in death.

A long time had passed. Maya checked her wrist-watch and got a bit of a shock to see that it was already five minutes past midnight.

'Maya . . .' she heard someone uttering her name. She turned around to find Amol standing there. Amol looked slightly older than the last time Maya saw him in college, which was more than six years ago. But he still appeared so gallant—in his teal-coloured hoodie with CK printed on it and jeans and his grey CK shoes. He looked like someone who had just had a *Calvin Klein* makeover.

'What are you doing here?' she demanded.

'I am making a video. For my Instagram.'

'Right. But at this hour? It's a bit absurd.' Maya snapped as she was puzzled.

Amol was her boyfriend in college. Maya had broken up with him because he was extra-protective and possessive. Maya was a pushover for the seven months she spent with him before she got fed up. She had told herself at the time that she was nobody's puppet and will not take it anymore.

Amol smiled and justified himself, 'I don't have a choice now. This is strictly business. 95,000 followers don't care about my safety. They need entertainment. I am hoping for 1 million followers soon. I don't know if you have seen my profile. My Instagram handle is—Amolville.'

'I can imagine how hard it must be. Getting paid to post on social media could be such a pain. Probably you should switch over to something less challenging like the military, Amol.' Maya shrugged her shoulders off.

Amol replied, looking at his watch, 'Mock me all you want. Being an Instagram influencer is a real thing, and it has worked wonders for me. Regardless, people always belittle it. But—right now I am a bit concerned about you being here at this hour. . .'

'It might be risky for pretty girls. Nobody is going to harm *me*. Anyway, thanks for your concern. I was here to attend a party. I am going home now.' Maya lied and turned away from Amol and his camera and started walking away.

Amol ran up to her and said, 'Hey, you are wrong. I always thought you were pretty. Care for a selfie? For old time's sake? I might get many of our college friends to follow me if I post a picture with you. May I, Maya, please!'

Maya knew that Amol was just trying to make her feel good, but he was unaware of her plight. Despite this, she thought that since she was going to be dead soon, it didn't matter. She would die in peace after making someone happy, even if it were for a little while. Who knows, her death might even come in highly useful to Amol to acquire more emotional followers. She unwittingly agreed to his proposal.

After thirty minutes of Amol posting the selfie with Maya tagged, Maya was almost ready to give up walking and do what she had planned to do—when out of the blue her phone started buzzing with Instagram notifications. There were 300 of those in less than thirty minutes!

As she opened her account, she had 190 *likes* on the selfie posted by Amol and 110 following *requests*. His caption was: 'Bumping into an ex, and having no hard feelings is the best feeling in the world.'

She couldn't believe her eyes. Quite a few reasons had contributed to Maya's decision to end her life. The most crucial being—lack of self-confidence—and per perceived feeling of not receiving any attention from anyone, whatsoever. And there it was. All the attention was coming to her with just one random *selfie.*

This made Maya stop for a minute and reconsider her decision. Her mind started racing over the bitter memories of her past.

Maya always considered herself unlucky and flawed in many ways. She thought of herself as short (short enough to be called names), dark (dark-enough to get *fairness* advice from everyone on the go), and fat (fat enough to be invisible to guys). All three are said to be the fundamentals of a woman's beauty, in the eyes of beholders. More so in contemporary Indian society. The colloquial slangs such as *moti (meaning fat)*, *kaali (meaning black)* and *chhoti (meaning little)* have been so much in circulation that they come out of people's mouth in the most secure seatings. For example, siblings call each other with such names or fairness creams for both, and women are high selling products into the market since the beginning of time. Believe it or not, even newborn babies get to be judged on a scale of whiteness or blackness from 0 to 10. From the photoshopped waistlines to the superiority of fairer skin tones in life to the evolution of heels, things got so out of control that it took the basic humanity out of the pool. Maya wasn't the only one who faced the music.

But for Maya, no matter how hard she refused to be cowed down and tried to fight these demons in her mind valiantly because of her incredible insight and sharp intellect. It was difficult for her to deal with how she thought others perceived her. She ultimately gave up.

Getting bullied over her physical appearance was not unusual for Maya—at every age, front and platform. At the tender age of ten, Maya's mother tried to help her *friendless* daughter in every possible way. She organized play-dates with a couple of people who had children of a similar age-group. Every time Maya would end up acting up in the presence of other parents and children, on being called a *lazy cow* or a *fatso* or an *ugly panda*.

Then, a ray of hope came into Maya's life with a new friend. When she was fifteen, Maya met Nafisa—one of her new classmates and her bench-partner in school. Their mothers knew each other through the local community. Nafisa's family had just moved into the neighbourhood.

Nafisa's height was that of a skyscraper in comparison to Maya's. She had amber-coloured eyes on top of a skinny, fair-complexioned body. To Maya, Nafisa appeared friendly and genuine. She had asked, 'Maya, I like you. Plus I am new here. Will you be my friend?' As they became close friends, Maya was happy, more confident than ever before. Nafisa grew fond of her and would sit with her during lunch-breaks. The two girls were seen bonding, fully immersed like there was no tomorrow.

Maya had realized by then that Nafisa was kind-hearted, but she wasn't as sharp. As a good friend, Maya helped Nafisa with her school assignments.

A couple of weeks later, there was an announcement at school about an essay-writing competition on a topic of personal choice. Maya got overly excited and started exploiting every source in the library. She finally decided to pick her topic. Her essay was titled: *Being ugly is brutal.*

Maya had written about her life. She had explained about the terrifying psychological effects of getting bullied due to appearance.

She had researched and used real examples of lifetime complications faced by bullied people. She had also included a couple of paragraphs on people who had to put in a load of extra efforts to climb the same ladder as their bullies, distracting them from their primary goals. It was a great essay. Nafisa curiously read it and declared: 'It's outstanding. You must participate.'

Maya scoffed. She then opened her heart to her friend, 'I have stage fright. I can't read it out to the entire class full of staring eyes. So, would you read it out for me?' Nafisa knew how vulnerable Maya was and gladly agreed to do the job.

At the competition, Nafisa was all set to read Maya's essay with her eloquent delivery. She read the entire piece in one go and finished it by saying, 'Those were my heartfelt words as I want to challenge the temperament that segregates the beautiful from the ugly. *I, Nafisa Singh, have written this essay dedicated to my best friend, Maya.'*

Nafisa received accolades and won the competition. Maya, deeply shocked, never spoke to her after the betrayal. She was used to being called names all of her school life. She would bear the humiliation and criticism. But what Nafisa had done after befriending her and infiltrating her private emotions, was beyond her imagination.

Maya made it through high school with a good score (enough to get into a Bachelor of Commerce, honours degree at Delhi University.) She believed that this was a slap on the face of all the people who bullied and outcasted her until then—the kids at school, the passive-aggressive relatives, the boys who gave her the side-eye, the teachers who agreed to disagree with her helplessness, and lastly, predators like Nafisa, who dehumanized Maya and took away from her something they didn't deserve.

Maya had a great time in college. She mostly kept to herself but was good in subjects like English and Accounts. She even managed to make a couple of friends discreetly. She even went on stage. She was approached by her crush Amol at the college festival after she delivered the opening speech. They went out for a coffee and then another one and then yet another one before they started dating. After their break-up, Maya was relieved and focused on herself.

Maya subsequently did a post-grad degree and joined the corporate sector. In contrast, Amol joined theatre and ultimately became a social media influencer. Nevertheless, Maya's job was good enough to provide her with all the material comforts she expected. This wasn't good enough to last long. As she turned 23, Maya started facing the brutal world again when everyone around her suddenly got worried about, '*Who is going to marry her*?'

She was forced to diet, join the gym and put on a new face pack every day. 'Well! We can't do anything about your height but at least we can try and fix your weight and your complexion,' Maya's mom said to her repeatedly. But despite the efforts, nothing changed.

Maya's mother made Maya wear her navy and scarlet colour-combination kalamkari saree, every time a matchmaking meeting was scheduled. She would tell Maya, 'This saree looks beautiful on you. It seems that it was made for you.'

Arranged marriage in India is a bit like speed dating. Eighteen boys came to Maya's house within six months, and each of them turned Maya down. Yes, she was rejected by eighteen boys, seven of whom were obese, twelve of them were professionally unsettled, and five of them were above the age of forty. Maya was devastated. This created an atmosphere that resembled mourning over a death in the house. She cried for nights, wanting to run away from the misery. She kept blaming herself for not trying hard enough to rectify her flaws. Finally, Maya made up her mind to commit suicide.

But the mind that had decided on suicide was now completely blown away by Amol's Instagram post, with added filters that made a big difference in Maya's appearance. Moreover, the appreciation that followed was unbelievable. She began reading the comments and inferred that Amol was right about social media. They were full of positivity.

'Maya looks dapper.'

'I am a big fan of Maya.'

'Such a beauty she is.'

'Why did you ever break up with her?'

'Her face is glowing.'

'You go girl.'

'Proud of you, Maya. You have come a long way.'

'She's a sweetheart.'

Maya was in shock. But she felt surprisingly delighted. She felt a tide of euphoria and the desire for more started emerging inside the dead sea of her heart. She was in a fix. The paradox of the situation was that what Maya had always been fighting with, was now making her happy.

This made her think. Maya put the decision to commit suicide at bay and decided to give a try to follow the path she had just discovered, to enjoy the benefits of social media engagement. She took a selfie and made a zillion filter adjustments and posted it with the caption: *Admiring myself, thanks to @amolville for a great selfie.*

Lo and behold, she immediately gained eighty-nine more followers. Tagging Amol in her post, worked wonders for Maya. Accidentally, she had stumbled upon something which immediately got her the attention she needed. She acknowledged the signal and decided to pursue the path circumstances had bestowed upon her.

This was enough for Maya to become an addict. She started posting photos of herself wearing weird clothes, doing anything awkward, forgetting her earlier routine. Plus, she came up with a great caption every time and voila! It worked wonders for Maya.

Now Maya had a well-planned social media rigmarole which she had inculcated in her life. Her strategies to fake her life were thoroughly organized and aptly executed. She would wake up early in the morning and go to the terrace and get clicked with a yoga pose or with dumbbells, and water droplets on her face pretending it as sweat. She would post this with captions about working out. And after this, she would go back to bed.

She started bluffing people with fake food habits. She would take water in a tall glass, add a few drops of watercolour, green or purple, and add a few drops of foam using dish soap. She did this every day to post a picture with a caption like an aloe drink or spinach drink or beets or dragon fruit. And after this, she would eat junk food.

Maya faked love. She googled: *tricks to create a make-believe boyfriend for Instagram purposes*. She started pretending to be holding hands with or sharing a drink with two straws in the same glass by getting her mom to do it all and just capturing the required portion and disguising it with photo filters.

She had apps that made her appear slimmer, taller and fairer. She even had magical apps that made her look as if she were wearing makeup, jewellery and any kind of hair-style in the world that Maya desired.

Maya started faking her heart out too. She became an opportunist for social media posts. She used the misery of others to create posts with an emotional pull. If she saw a disabled beggar, she posted: *life is tough but be grateful for what you have*. If it were an injured or dead bird, she posted: *my heart goes out to this*. And then, as usual, she would just move on with her life in search of the next post.

Then came the time when paid marketing campaigns started falling into her lap. She gained followers and money. She started faking her life on social media to the extent that she began losing touch with reality, so much so that Maya spent fourteen to sixteen hours a day doing it. By the end of two years, Maya had become a real social media addict who had completely lost touch with the non-virtual aka real world.

Maya became delusional, utterly oblivious of the monstrous effects social media addiction was having on her. She started to believe that she looked just like the person in her social media photos. She had thousands of friends and followers on the internet, but none in reality. Indeed, none of the social media friends knew what Maya was in real life.

As the proverb goes, 'As you sow, so you shall reap.' Maya too had to become a martyr of her own life choices.

One fine morning, Maya's mother asked her to give social media a break and accompany her to her sister's house. Maya refused as usual since she had stopped entirely seeing people, to follow her social media addiction. 'Stop sneaking around. You are nosy. I don't pry into your life, mom. You should stop doing it to me too.'

Maya's mother said, 'I know I am to blame to an extent for your downfall in the past, but right now, you are doing this to yourself. Why can't you just be my daughter for once? I don't care if you get married or not. I just want my daughter back.'

Maya sighed and responded in a condescending tone, 'Well! You think I will come to you as per your convenience. I am happy in what I am doing and wouldn't stop ever. The kind of love I am getting from my people is far above your fake motherly concern. And do you know, I have made Rs. 53.5 Lakhs from my social media in the short span of two years? Can you believe it? I know my preferences now. But none of it is for you. This is my revenge on you. A payback for undermining me all your life. You were nothing but a sadistic mother who tormented a vulnerable ugly daughter to the edge.'

Her mother was heart-broken. She started crying and said, 'I wish I had said something sooner to prevent you from being so strongly in denial. I am not proud of myself. All I did was shape you in becoming needy and selfish at the same time.' Maya was so cynical and eccentric now that her mother felt she had no choice but to give up.

The mother shared with her sister the concern for Maya's addiction. Her sister told her the adverse effects Maya's condition could have if left untreated. Maya's mother rejected her sister's analysis of her situation as an impasse. After a long session of conversation and arguments, the sisters decided to get Maya to consult a therapist. With a heavy heart and an overly anxious motherly mind, Maya's mom returned from her sister's house.

However, she met with a road accident on the way. She was hit by a red Maruti Suzuki Swift Dzire and ended up with a ruptured spleen and an extensive amount of internal bleeding, enough to cost her life. The police reached Maya's house and gave her the bad news. The driver of the car was arrested.

Maya was deeply affected by her mother's death. She didn't speak to any of the people who visited her house to express their grief and condolences. Maya's mother's last words to her echoed in her mind like a refrain. She couldn't stop having visions of her mom repeating her last words to her 'I'm not proud of myself' over and over again.

After the funeral the next day, Maya started facing withdrawal symptoms because of her separation from technology. She decided to check her phone and went inside her room and locked the door. She got the shock of her life because three hundred of her followers had dropped because of her two days' inactivity. She felt shortness of breath and began panting. Her scalp started sweating profusely and her hands began shaking slightly. She knew it was her FOMO of social media taking over her grief of losing her mother. She was petrified. She said to herself, 'Maya, you snooze, you lose!'

She quickly decided to post about her dead mom to regain followers through sympathy. To her utter shock, she found that she did not have a single picture of her mom in the zillion camera folders. She put on a white top and took a selfie with fake tears and again, used a thousand filters to look like the fake Maya as always, and then posted it with the caption: *Lost my mom two days ago. Can't stop crying.*

The post worked wonders for her. In the next twenty minutes, Maya gained five hundred sympathetic followers from all over the world. Her phone started flooding with condolences. It seemed that her mother had died on social media yet again. And finally, Maya began to become normal.

Just then, Maya realized that she had missed out on reading the comments on her post since the day of her mother's death where she had posted a sensual photo of her in a body-hugging, red cocktail dress from Guess, black high heels from Steve Madden and make-up goods from Mac. She looked flawless in the picture, courtesy photo-editing apps. The caption she had posted was: *Date number four, who knows what's in store*?

After the post, Maya had carefully packed away the dress and the shoes, to be exchanged for new ones for free, as she was a social celebrity by now, endorsing brands through her posts.

She scrolled down all the 988 comments and came back to one, which was posted at 4.45 p.m., the exact time of her mother's death, two days ago. A boy posted the comment. Maya saw his name was Tejas. Maya was appalled to realize that it was the same name that the police had disclosed, about the person who was being accused of hitting Maya's mother.

She went through the social profile of Tejas, only to find out that he, indeed, drove the same car that hit her mother, as described by the police. She couldn't believe what she had done to her mother. She had told her mother, just before her death, that she preferred social media over her love.

The irony of the situation was that the driver of the car at fault had Maya's latest Instagram post open on his phone screen where he had just finished commenting '*You are an inspiration, Maya,*' while driving, and hitting her mother; and ultimately killing her. Maya said to herself, 'Losing my mother like this serves me well.'

Maya pledged that very moment to quit faking her life. She took a photo of herself and without any filters and editing, shared it with the world, along with the story of her mother's death. Below the photograph, she wrote: *The accident isn't responsible for killing my mother. I am. Here, I am introducing the real me to you today. I don't need anyone's approval to make myself feel worthy. And neither do you!*

Six months later, Maya had completed a meditation therapy, achieved a clear head and empowered her better side. She donated all the money she had earned as a media influencer to social media de-addiction centres. She created awareness among the youth; schools and colleges invited her to give talks about the adverse effects of social media. She organized campaigns, street plays, wrote banners and brochures and also spread the word through her Facebook and Instagram accounts. She took her audience in confidence: 'Are you suffering from Obsessive Compulsive Disorder?''Are you trapped in a negative way of thinking?''Are you fretting about snapping out of it?' She suggested various strategies to get out of this repeatedly-occurring malady. She cautioned people with a warning: 'New Technology: Handle it with care.' Her life was now fully dedicated to the 'social media de-addiction'. But her motto was self-love and her tagline on every front was: *You need nobody's approval.*

Maya was invited to present a paper in the plenary session at the 31st Psychology International Conference, held in New Delhi. An entire day was dedicated to social media addiction. Maya's experience was a valuable one to share.

Maya reached the venue wearing her mother's unique *kalamkari saree* and began speaking thus: 'Good morning, one and all. My name is Maya, and I am here to share my cautionary tale.'

Her presentation was adjudged best in the conference.

A Tale of Two Sisters

As Ananya entered Ridhi's room and watched her sleep peacefully, she couldn't control the rush of emotions running through her blood. She stood there for precisely 15 minutes, looking at her twin sister. Ananya closed her subtly-smoked grey eyelids with tears rolling down her prominent and contoured cheekbones, all the way down her pink blushed cheeks. Ananya had neat wavy hair—coloured half brunette and half blonde with the perfect balayage. She carried her toned body on 4-inches peep-toe heels in a graceful posture and looked prettier than ever while she stood and cried next to Ridhi's bed.

The very next moment, Ananya took out a tissue paper from her gold *Chanel* sling that was hanging diagonally from her left shoulder down to her right hip bag to wipe her tears. She took her sister's right hand and kissed it while letting more tears fall from her eyes. She picked the pillow that was lying on the floor and pushed it on to Ridhi's face, covering her mouth and nose and forcing it down so vigorously that Ridhi started to struggle, as much as she possibly could. Ananya closed her eyes to avoid looking at Ridhi battling for breath while trying to kill her sister. And just after a few more seconds, Ridhi stopped struggling and lay there with eyes closed, and as she breathed her last, it was over. Ananya opened her eyes and removed the cushion to see her dead sister's face.

The shenanigans began 25 years ago as soon as first Ridhi, and fifteen minutes later, Ananya were born. 'My two little precious dolls,' said their father to their mother.

Ridhi and Ananya had a peculiar childhood. The identical twins' mother wanted to be a doctor and not what she ended up becoming—a housewife when she was young. She firmly believed that if her parents had brought her up in a way where she understood competition, she would have become one. She never understood the need to beat her peers to be successful and hence simply focused on improving herself. Their father fully agreed with their mother, and together, the couple pledged to make their daughters win all the races in life. The father got a framed poster for their house saying: *A horse never runs so fast as when he has other horses to catch up and outpace.* As the girls started their journey as parents, the competition-driven parents started comparing their daughters to each other.

Ananya and Ridhi's soon-to-be-miserable lives began with the constant compulsive need of trying to prove themselves. Even as babies! The parents had a baby book each for Ananya and Ridhi and recorded everything religiously. Who got the first tooth, who crawled first, which one of the two sisters ate a new vegetable, which one took the first step before the other, who spoke first and who spoke better first, so on and so forth. The worst part was that the parents made it explicit to the girls by repeatedly enforcing the point that one was somehow superior to the other.

'Ananya, your sister, stopped wearing diapers two weeks ago, and you are still not able to catch up with her. It is such a shame.'

'Ridhi, Ananya is taking such good care of her white fairy dress while you have a chocolate stain. You are both five years old today, and she is far superior to you in taking care of belongings.'

By the time the girls began their schooling, they had already developed a sense of competition and believed that they had to beat each other at every task.

'I finished my phonics worksheet before Ananya.'

'I got an A and Ridhi got a B in our Art project.'

The competitive spirit between the sisters was only getting worse with time. The urge to beat each other in every task seemed like an effective way to enhance performance, but the parents had no clue about the damage it was causing to the girls.

'I got selected for the inter-school debate competition, but Ananya did not.'

'I beat Ridhi in Art class again.'

As they grew up to become adolescents, they had a sense of animosity towards each other.

'You don't even know when to use *your* and when *you're,* Ananya. How are you my sister?'

'I am puzzled. I got my first period before you, but you are older. Puberty chose me over you, Ridhi.'

'How could you be so dumb, Ananya? Integration and differentiation is basic math.'

'I haven't seen any person as lazy as you, Ridhi. I won the swimming championship while you were sleeping all day.'

And then as they entered teenage, they waged an ugly war. The twins were both happy in their individual lives, but their sibling rivalry pulled them apart. They despised and antagonized each other at every possible opportunity they got.

'I am prettier than you. You are just a fat and lazy sloth wearing sweatpants, lucky enough to have my face, Ridhi.'

'I am going to burst that bubble for you soon Ananya when we get our high school scores. I will crack all tests and get into some great college, and you are just going to be found in a ditch, probably drunk, or rather overdosed with *heroin.*' Ananya felt that Ridhi had crossed a boundary and was furious at her hateful comment. It was the worst thing Ridhi had ever said to her, and it added fuel to the fire.

A couple of days later, Ridhi was in the shower, and Ananya was looking for her iPad inside the study desk at home when she found a notification appear on Ridhi's phone:

Cool, see you at five there.

Parag.

Ananya got curious and couldn't help herself from intruding her sister's privacy and opening her text message exchanges with Parag. She began to read them with shock:

I've been meaning to ask you out for a few days now.

Parag

Ditto!

Ridhi.

Wow! Unbelievable. I'm so happy.

Parag.

I am flattered. I've had a crush on you for a year.

Ridhi

Join me for coffee after school?

Parag.

Ananya was shocked to see Ridhi getting asked out and also still vehemently enraged with what she had said to her the last time. She decided to settle scores with her sister. She deleted Parag's latest text from Ridhi's phone and thought of an evil plan.

Ananya went outside and stealthily called Parag and asked him to meet her. She spent a few hours with him before returning home to her sister.

'Hello, Ms *Virgin* Ridhi. I just slept with a guy, and now he loves me to the brink. I feel sorry for you', Ananya said to Ridhi.

'What the hell, Ananya? Where were you? Who were you with?' Ridhi panicked.

'Do you know the guy named Parag at our school? I was with him in his mom's car. It was so passionate and sensual,' Ananya looked into Ridhi's eyes and kept her hands on her shoulders.

'What are you saying? Are you out of your mind, Ananya?'

'Shhhhh Ridhi! Revenge is best served cold. I know you had a crush on him. But let's be honest, you are just not attractive. I, on the other hand, am cute as a Disney princess and just lost my virginity to the guy of your dreams.'

'Don't you worry about me, Ananya. I might be a virgin, but at least I am educated enough to protect myself from STDs and even worse, pregnancy. I hope you don't get one of those.' Ridhi reinforced her concerns in an utterly bitter manner. She was angry. She couldn't believe the height of atrocity Ananya had jumped caused her just to get back at her. She justified it with Ananya's negligence and immaturity. Regardless, she was still more concerned about her sister.

Events unfolded darkly, and the worst possible probability took its form. Ananya was pregnant at the age of sixteen. She found out at six p.m. that day and hadn't stepped out of her bedroom, which she shared with Ridhi. She didn't know what to do except cry in bed.

'So the predator fell prey. See the realities of being irresponsible. I am ashamed of you, Ananya.' Ridhi whispered in Ananya's ear.

'But how did you know, Ridhi?' Ananya had no clue.

'I know your cycle. You never used any sanitary pads this month, and that's why I checked the trash bin in the bathroom. The pregnancy test kit spoke for itself. What are you going to do now?' Ridhi's voice was full of compassion. She was worried about her sister.

'I'll figure something out. Since when do you care, Ridhi?'

'I know we both wish otherwise, but I am your sister. I have to get you out of this mess', said Ridhi while tucking herself in her bed, next to Ananya. Ananya sobbed the entire night softly.

The next morning, Ridhi took Ananya to an abortion clinic while keeping the entire matter under wraps. Ananya was guilty of trying to bulldoze Ridhi. While the procedure was taking place, Ridhi sat next to Ananya, holding her hand. For the first time in life, Ananya felt grateful to have Ridhi as her sister.

'I thought you'd hate me even more after this', Ananya said to Ridhi after a week of the incident.

'I do. What you did to me was vicious. But you are my sister at the end of the day. You even look just like me. I can't avoid you even if I wanted to. Besides, a family always sticks together. You know how they say that blood is thicker than water and all.'

'Touché!' said Ananya as the sisters giggled and hugged each other.

Everything was over in an instant, and soon enough, their lives went back to normal. Their sibling rivalry took a beautiful twist and transformation into true sisterly love. Despite that, the repulsive debacle continued between them, but only to help make each other's life better.

At the age of 23, Ridhi had just finished her MBBS degree, and Ananya was working as an assistant stylist at a high profile fashion boutique.

'I got into a postgraduate degree. I picked Obstetrics and Gynecology. What did Ananya get? What is she even doing with her life?'

'I'm happy that my sister is becoming a gynaecologist but don't you undermine me, Ridhi.'

'Why don't you just get married if you are not interested in a career?' Ridhi despised Ananya not taking her career seriously.

'On that note, I want you to know that I wish to open a boutique store of my own now', said Ananya and her parents agreed to help her. Ridhi was finally happy for her sister and gave her a smile of pride.

Ananya's boutique was ready within no time. Ananya was an exemplary fashion stylist, and on the very first day of opening, she got her first customer. It was Ridhi. She looked around the store and brought clothes to the counter, enough to fill a full wardrobe for herself. Ananya grabbed her sister's hand and pulled her close to hug her tightly. 'Thanks, sis. I didn't know you loved me that much. And I love you too. You can count on me for anything. I promise you that I will never say no.'

These incidents deepened the relationship between Ananya and Ridhi. They became each other's confidants.

'I need you to meet Kunal. I've been dating him for a long time now, and I like him a lot, Ridhi. How about lunch with him? Is tomorrow ok?' Ananya asked Ridhi with heartfelt desperation and excitement. She was somehow looking for Ridhi's approval of Kunal before things got more serious with Kunal. Ridhi agreed.

'Kunal and I will pick you up from your hospital for lunch tomorrow.'

Showing concern, Ridhi said, 'I am extremely nervous about you two getting along forever. I'm keeping my fingers crossed.'

Next day, Ananya and Kunal reached the hospital where Ridhi worked as promised. Ridhi had texted Ananya about a delay of 20 minutes, and she decided to have a cup of coffee with Kunal while she waited for her sister in the canteen.

An old lady and a man in his late twenties came to her table and sat next to her. Ananya felt a bit awkward because another table was empty, just next to them.

The man started, 'Dr. Ridhi, this is my mother. I wanted her to meet the baby. Will that be ok?'

Ananya understood. 'I am not Dr. Ridhi. I am her twin sister.'

The man didn't seem to believe Ananya, and just then Ridhi came over.

'Phew! I was so confused, Dr. Ridhi. You two are twins indeed', said the man with a smile.

Ridhi sighed and then said, 'Look, Mahesh, It's perfectly fine that you want your mother to see your newborn daughter. But she doesn't even remember who *you* are. How is she going to relate to your baby daughter? You are putting too much pressure on yourself, and I don't want you to get your heartbroken when she doesn't exactly show a grandmother's excitement over there.'

Mahesh had tears in his eyes. He said, 'Dr. Ridhi, she will always be my mother. She's all I've got. My wife and I have dedicated our lives to my mother's dementia. We can't just give up on her.'

Ridhi scoffed and took Mahesh's hand and said, 'No matter how strongly you believe or wish for, your mother's condition won't improve. I have talked to other doctors too. I just wish you could move on with your life now. Your wife and baby are waiting for you, and you haven't seen them since I delivered your baby. Please go and be the husband and be the father you need to be right now. Your wife has had a traumatic delivery. She needs you.'

Mahesh left with her mother, leaving Ridhi, Kunal, and Ananya behind.

'That was so sad, Ridhi. I don't know how you deal with all this. But it is such a dilemma to let your loved one just disappear from your life. Especially because it's not like they are dead, they are still around but are more of a liability', said Ananya in an intriguing tone.

'You know, Ananya, since I get to meet such people every day, I strongly believe that people should have a right to choose to die in these cases. I have seen patients who beg doctors to kill them!' Ridhi exclaimed.

Kunal intervened, 'That's inhumane, Ridhi. You are a doctor, for heaven's sake.'

'You don't understand. I mean, for example, a brain-dead patient or dementia patient or a quadriplegic patient or someone who is terminally ill and has no hope for improvement deserves to decide on their own. It's immoral to force them to live a hopeless and meaningless life where they have no freedom, no flexibility, no consent, no choice, and their lives are all about the people around them.'

Kunal said, 'When you put it that way, Ridhi, it makes a lot more sense. I had no idea. I think I have no option but to agree.'

Ridhi said with a deep voice, 'I would die every day and every minute deep inside my heart if I have to lead such a lifeless life with the unexplainable and worst of all, inconvincible pain and suffering.'

'So according to you, these people should be killed? Either at their own will or by the consent of their relatives if they aren't fit enough to decide. But they deserve to die. Agree to disagree!' Ananya sounded displeased.

'Ananya, you haven't seen the kind of physical and emotional trauma such people go through each day of their lives. Euthanasia is legal in quite a few scenarios, in countries like the Netherlands, Belgium and a couple more. This is something about which I feel strongly. If tomorrow something happens to me, and I am at such a stage where I am so dependent on you for even a sip of water, I would want to end my miserable life. I am not saying everyone should want the same. It's just what I want,' Ridhi justified.

'Anyway. You are right here, and you are perfectly healthy, Ridhi. So, let's go and eat now', said Ananya dismissing the topic.

A few days later, Kunal invited Ananya over to spend a weekend away with him at a resort on the outskirts. She let Ridhi know and left.

Ananya knew what Kunal was after. Hence she had packed her beautiful peach off-shoulder dress, pink peep-toe heels, and her entire makeup kit. She took a while to get dressed when Kunal asked her to go for dinner. She looked divine.

Kunal surprised Ananya with a marriage proposal. Ananya said yes, and they got engaged. And she couldn't wait to let her sister know.

She took her phone out to call her and saw 29 missed calls from her mother and panicked. She called back and heard her mother's horrified voice, 'Ananya, your sister got stabbed by a roadside *junkie* . . . she had removed his wife's ruptured endometriosis uterus. She fell and hit her head. Come back, please.'

Ananya asked in a profoundly puzzled voice, 'But Ridhi must have consented to the man before the procedure on his wife. Didn't she?'

'The man was high on drugs, Ananya. Hence the patient's father signed the consent form in an emergency. The husband is back to his senses now, and the first thing he heard was that he wouldn't be able to have children because Ridhi removed his wife's uterus.' Ananya's mother nearly choked with the crying and talking.

Ananya rushed back to see her sister. She couldn't stop seeing flashes of the recent great times they both had been spending together. She reached the hospital and rushed in as quickly as she possibly could. Her mother was crying on the bench, and she saw her mother's lips move as she read them from a distance. She could only make out: *spinal cord injury and quadriplegia*.

Ananya's soul seemed to have left her body. She felt a vacuum emerge inside her. Her blood stopped flowing, and she felt though her limbs were transformed into huge rocks which couldn't move.

Ananya's father came to her. He hugged her, and they both cried their hearts out.

'Dad, when is she going to recover? Can we do something?'

'She will never recover, darling. We have lost your sister's body forever.'

'That's not possible. It was just one incident. How can it have such a result?'

'It is a spinal cord injury. Face it, Ananya. Ridhi is going to be quadriplegic forever.'

'I don't accept that. Just one stab and she can never walk? Or even use her hands? Or her body? Dad, are you saying that she can't do anything ever? She's going to be miserable. How will she survive?'

'At least we still have her. She could have died. We could have lost her.'

'And you think that would have been worse than this. I wish she were dead.'

Ananya's father was shocked. 'I know we didn't raise you two the right way. I know you both hate each other because of us. But your sibling rivalry has gone too far. Your sister just escaped death with a slim chance of survival. Are you not happy that at least she is alive, Ananya?'

'Dad, wake up. She won't be able even to use the toilet. She can't even use her pelvic muscles for bowel movements. We have to . . . ugh! Ridhi will be dependent on us for every small task.'

'So, you have a problem with assisting her. You have nothing to worry about. You wouldn't have to lift a finger.' The father angrily responded.

Ananya's mother overheard the conversation and intervened, 'After all those years of comparison, I know who is a better human today. When Ridhi came to know about her condition, she told me about your visit to her hospital with Kunal. She was so happy for you. She asked me to remind you of what she had said to you that day before you begin your life with Kunal.' The mother sobbed profusely.

'What did she mean, mom?'

'She said you would know what to do,' said the mother.

Ananya started panting and collapsed on the floor. All she could now hear was what Ridhi had said to her at the hospital after meeting the dementia woman. She knew what Ridhi wanted. She had to make a decision, and it couldn't be delayed any further.

Hence Ananya went inside her sister's room. When Ananya picked up the pillow from the floor, she started shaking. Kunal followed her and came over to hold Ananya in his arms and whispered in her left ear, 'You know what she wants now. I will always love you, no matter what you decide.'

Ananya went ahead and killed Ridhi by suffocating her under the pillow. Their mother entered the room and yelled, 'What have you done, Ananya?'

Ananya said to her softly, 'I promised her that I would do whatever she asked me. I promised her that I would never say no.'

Paradigm Shift

'And the award for the Employee of the Year 2018 goes to—Samantha Joseph,' announced Prateek on the mic. He was Samantha's boyfriend and co-employee and was also the stage host for the event. Prateek and Samantha were at the annual corporate New Year's gala night of *New Delhi Money,* a financial consultancy firm. People gave a round of applause, and the spotlight fell on Samantha. She was sitting in her chair at one of the round tables amid her co-workers.

She had a big fat smile expressing her elation in full swing. She stood up gracefully like a celebrity and walked towards the stage to receive her award, a sleek bronze memento. Samantha raised the award, and her gang of friends began to pamper her by chanting, 'Sam the queen, Sam, the queen. . .'

Prateek went merry on the mic: 'Congratulations, Samantha! You deserve this.'

Samantha gleefully smiled, took off the mic from Prateek and addressed the crowd like a newly crowned champion, 'I'm delighted at the honour bestowed on me. As the great Dalai Lama has said, *if you think you are too small to make a difference, try sleeping with a mosquito*. I want to thank and accredit the one person who made my smallness big—my mother, my angel who made me believe in myself. I am what I am today because of her. Ladies and gentlemen, I am deeply overwhelmed and highly obliged to all of you for being here. I hope I can keep this up.'

While walking down the steps, Samantha had a fall, and her award rolled over only to end up under one of the audience's chairs. A waiter who was serving drinks abandoned his tray and came to the rescue. He first helped Samantha get up and then lied down on the floor to pick the award. His hand crawled underneath the chairs, digging in between people's feet. The people around were Samantha's colleagues at work, but they did virtually nothing to retrieve her award. The courtesy shown by the waiter moved Sam. She thanked him with a handshake.

The waiter got startled and joined his hands in a namaste gesture instead. He laughed nervously and said, 'No problem. I am just doing my job, madam.'

Sam thought to herself: *It seems it is a crime to be poor or uneducated because people treat you like crap. Only if all the privileged helped the underprivileged as my mom did, the world would be a better place to live. All people seem to be entitled corporate creeps here.*

Sam was an adopted child. Her adoption was discreetly demarcated because of the striking incidental differences in facial features due to the different ethnic origins between her parents and herself. She had a wheatish complexion and a little face. She had a sharp nose and long beautiful eyelashes. Sam's parents were fair-skinned, tall and had relatively smaller eyes. Sam was adopted from an orphanage in Delhi: her parents were from the East of India, Assam. However, she was in good hands, and her life had turned a new leaf after adoption.

Sam's parents were firm believers in "Education is key to life. "Ever since Sam was a little girl, the entire emphasis of her upbringing was on her education. She never received a non-educational birthday present or a non-educational birthday party for that matter. Her family outings had been to Science fairs, Mathematics fun parks, libraries, museums and historical monuments with intensive guided tours. While at it, Sam had to carry notebooks and pens in her backpack and take notes. She devotedly followed her parents' directions and searched for her ideal career path.

Sam loved her life. She was proud of her parents and their way of upbringing her. Their teachings helped her achieve everything she ever wanted. She did excellent in school, college and her post-graduation. Sam's thorough approach and planning based on extensive research and number crunching led her to pick a career in finance. All this was followed by an extensive interview and well-deserved job with a reputed concern at *New Delhi Money*.

For the celebration of Sam winning the award, Prateek had a party planned at their apartment, straight after the ceremony. Their group of close friends came over along with a few other people. There was plenty of food and drinks everywhere. There were karaoke and dancing.

Sam loved having people over. Her live-in maid Pinky was 27 years old with a relatively fair complexion but had a massive birthmark on top of her left cheekbone. This birthmark could be removed, only if Pinky had the money.

But making lemonade out of a life full of lemons, 'Birthmark Pinky' was a terrific housekeeper and an unbeatable cook. Sam had nothing to worry about because

Pinky would take care of all the food and the mess after the party.

At the party, one of the office colleagues, Priyanka asked Sam about her and Prateek's story.

'I shifted to Delhi three years ago when I got this job. I moved in with Prateek 6 months ago after having been in a relationship with him for over five months.'

Priyanka was in her late thirties and had two teenage daughters at home. She asked Sam about Pinky and if she knew any other good maid like her since she was looking for one. Priyanka stated, 'I want someone who is educated at least up to middle school because otherwise, they don't know what they are doing. My last maid didn't know how to use a water-boiling kettle as she couldn't read the words—CAUTION and HOT written in big and bold letters on top of it. She ended up burning her hand, and I FIRED her.' Priyanka started laughing like a maniac and said, 'Pun intended!'

Sam got creeped out with cruelty and then the audacity to show it off. She dismissed the conversation politely before she had to hear another word from Priyanka who always seemed to be ready to belittle and ridicule people. She continued to play hostess along with Prateek upfront, while Pinky took care of everything in the background. The time was 1 a.m. Veronica, Sam's friend, got drunk and ended up vomiting on the carpet. Prateek and Sam were disgusted but Pinky helped Veronica to the bathroom.

One of the guests said, 'Yuck! Why did you eat so many of Sam's delicious prawns if you just had to throw them up?' Everybody laughed.

'They were indeed delicious, Sam,' said another person.

Prateek responded, 'Thanks a lot. This is Sam's mom's recipe. But our maid Pinky is a great cook. She is a great asset.'

'Oh, Prateek. You are so naive. It is all Sam and her mom's magic. Given Sam's mother has never even met Pinky!! Pinky is just doing what she is being told. Sam's mother is the creator. Sam brought her legacy and forwarded it to your maid. Cheers to her for teaching a maid so well. And to your mom, Sam,' said Priyanka.

Sam had never had to deal with the domestic help before as her mother took care of everything. Moreover, Sam was a responsible and self-reliant person who took care of all her tasks. After putting Veronica to bed in the guest bedroom, Pinky returned and took the stinky carpet outside on the veranda and started washing it with a hose and some laundry detergent.

Sam noticed her and ran up to her. 'Pinky, you don't need to wash that. It can be thrown away. I don't expect you to wash off other people's vomit.'

'It is OK, madam. I will clean it so nicely that it wouldn't emit any smell. I have cleaned my father's drunken vomit all my life. Leave it to me.'

She soaked the carpet with a mixture of water, detergent and Dettol and left it out, to be scrubbed and rewashed in the morning.

All of a sudden lights were turned off, and Sam didn't know what was happening. A few candles were lit up. Then, Prateek took out a Tiffany box from the pocket of his jacket in front of everyone and sat down on one knee, next to Sam, who was taken by surprise.

Prateek kept looking into her eyes and started talking, 'Don't think that I am doing this because you look great today. It's because I love you. And the least I can say is that I am extremely proud of how far you have come and how legitimate everything about your accomplishments is. I love you for everything you've done. Will you marry me?'

Sam smiled with pride. 'Yes, Prateek. That will be great.' She said, and Prateek hugged her, and everyone clapped and screamed, 'HOORAY!'

After the party was over, everyone left. Sam went on to pick up the dirty dishes and Pinky came running to take them away from her. She said, 'Madam, I will do it. You sleep.'

In the bedroom, Samantha was taking her make-up off, and Prateek was in bed, reading a book. Sam couldn't help feeling sympathetic for Pinky.

'Poor Pinky! I think I am going to pay her extra for tonight. And did you hear what Priyanka said? She is so condescending. She fired her maid after she burnt her hand with hot water because she should have seen it coming. Pun intended! Such a bitch!'

Prateek began to laugh but was given the raging side-eye by Sam. 'What? Not everyone can think like you, honey. Your parents have brought you up to be so kind. Now please, stop fidgeting with your fingers; to bed now, fiancé. It's very late.'

Sam changed into her pyjamas and lied down next to Prateek. 'You know, Prateek, I feel that if people like Pinky had completed their education, they wouldn't have to face such deterrence. It is inevitable for her to be so naive. She cleans up vomit and other bodily excretions as if it were just a glass of spilt water. She has no idea what kind of risks she is putting herself to. She can't tell right from wrong. That's the exact reason why people turn to crime. I was reading an article the other day. . .'

'Whoa! I'm going to stop you right there. It's amazing how empathetic you are towards Pinky, sweetheart. But you've got to stop now. We just got engaged. I am happy is an understatement.'

'I am happy too. And I must say that I wasn't aware of your remarkable diamond picking skills. I have the four perfect Cs on my finger. There's the perfect brilliant round cut plus the 1.5 carats making it neither too big nor too small, plus the flawless and colourless neatly cut solitaire, sitting tight on the perfectly elegant platinum band. I love it.' Sam smiled as she held hands with Prateek.

'I think you should know that Veronica helped me pick the ring last week. It wasn't all me. She loves you a lot, Sam.'

They held hands after that and then both slept peacefully, dreaming about their future.

A week later, Sam's mother, Mrs. Mary Rose Joseph, visited her from Assam. She brought bags full of presents for Sam and Prateek. She got a bag full of traditional Assamese spices, pickles and an extravagant amount of household gifts. She bought an exclusive pure Assamese silk saree *mekhela chadar* and a pure gold necklace set and earrings which had intricate handmade flora and fauna of Assam in vibrant red and green for Sam as her engagement gift.

'This is so beautiful, Sam,' Prateek said as he felt the texture of the saree in his hands along with the gold jewellery set.

Pinky cleared up the unpacked luggage that mostly consisted of presents from the living room while Sam, Prateek, and Mrs. Joseph watched her.

'Pinky, please handle the stuff with care. It's very delicate,' cautioned Mrs. Joseph as she saw Pinky rushing with clearing up the tea set she had brought from a designer exhibition in Guwahati for Sam.

Pinky finally folded the silk saree neatly and took a long time to do it. It felt so delicate against her fingers that she wondered how it would feel against her body. And she froze at the moment she was about to give the saree its final fold.

'Pinky, are you alright? Please finish up quickly. Mom must be exhausted,' said Sam as she poked Pinky's shoulder.

Mrs. Joseph took the jewellery and the saree to her bedroom and locked it inside the cupboard safely so that Pinky wouldn't steal.

Sam had invited her friends over for lunch for her mother to meet them. They all were enjoying Mrs. Joseph's lip-smacking recipes, cooked by Pinky.

Everyone picked a spot to sit next to the couch, and Veronica sat on the carpet where she had vomited during the party. 'This is incredible, Sam. I can't tell that this carpet was thrown upon by me.' Veronica sighed.

Veronica then popped the question she had been longing to ask, 'I don't mean to pry aunty, but…'

Mrs Joseph replied, 'There were many challenges. I don't even know where to begin. When Sam's father and I got to know that we won't ever be able to have a baby of our own, we lost all hope. I faced clinical depression. It was the darkest time of our lives.'

'Mom, you don't have to say if you are uncomfortable,' said Sam as she saw her mother tearing up.

Mrs. Joseph smiled and shook her head in disapproval. She continued, 'My husband travelled a lot for work. I began to tag along whenever I could to cure my depression. Finally, the day came when I couldn't resist anymore. My desire to be a mother became my life, and we planned to adopt a child. We decided to adopt from Delhi because those days, Delhi was the fastest with paperwork.'

Veronica intervened with raised eyebrows, 'I understand, Aunty. But adopting a child could be a daunting experience. That must have been quite a challenge for you?'

'The challenging part was picking the child from the orphanage. Believe it or not, we had to choose the child out of four girls under the age of two. I am a human being, and hence I don't know any way to tell which child deserves a family more than the other. So, we picked the oldest of the four girls—Samantha, who was a mere twenty-month old.' Mrs. Joseph wiped away her tears as she sipped her tea.

Sam was in tears, and she hugged her mother.

Just then, Pinky walked in and took Mrs. Joseph's cup away in a tray she was carrying and Mrs. Joseph, while still hugging a sobbing Samantha, looked at Pinky's birthmark for a couple of seconds and then suddenly developed her eyes wide with shock. Her pious feelings took a hit, and some old skeletons began to peep out of the closet.

'Pinky, where are you from?' Mrs. Joseph asked most anxiously.

'I am from here, Madam. Delhi is my home since I can remember.'

'And that mark on your face, how did you get that?'

'It is a birthmark. It has always been there. I wish I could hide it, madam.'

'What about your family?' Mrs. Joseph asked Pinky as if she was interrogating her.

'I had a father who died of cancer a few years ago. Other than that, I don't have anyone except that I carry a terrible stroke of misfortune—like my facial birthmark.'

'Was he your birth father, Pinky?'

'Mom, what's the matter?' Sam expressed her curiosity about the fact that her mother was so much interested in a maid servant's life at such a tender moment.

'Just a second, Sam. Let me talk to her.' Mrs. Joseph turned towards Pinky again. 'Tell me, Pinky. Was he your birth father?'

Pinky was stunned, 'I don't know, madam. He loved me a lot, but I never met my mother, nor have I ever seen any pictures of her. He worked at an orphanage as a janitor, and I followed his footsteps. I became a cleaner too. He was very sick in the last ten years, so all I did was work.'

Mrs. Joseph confidently said, 'The name of the orphanage was—Asha and your father's name was—Ratan Singh Chaudhry. Am I right?'

Pinky nodded with her mouth wide open in shock.

'Mom, you have to tell me now. What do you know about this orphanage and Pinky?' Sam was feeling edgy with suspense.

Mrs. Joseph started sobbing loudly.

'Mom, you are scaring me. Tell me what's wrong?'

'Sam, listen to me as I would never repeat this. I was desperate to have a child, and your father and I became regular volunteers and donors of this orphanage—Asha. Pinky was always there with her father as Pinky's mother had passed away. We finally decided to take a child home after spending around two weeks visiting the orphanage regularly.'

Everyone looked askance at Mrs. Joseph now.

Pinky said, 'I always went to that place until around the age of nine when my father was diagnosed with some sort of stomach cancer. He tried his best to support me all those years. But he was just too distressed and sick. I had no choice except to become a maid. I had no schooling. I had to work as my ailing father needed medication and care. I had to bring food to the table plus clean up his mess. He spent the long excruciating ten long years like that. Sometimes, I just wished while going to sleep that when I wake up in the morning, my father was dead. I loved him a lot, Madam. But I became sick of it. And one day, it happened, and I finally became free.'

Sam looked scornfully at Pinky, and said, 'I don't know what to say Pinky. You had undoubtedly a terrible life, but your father had a worse life than you. And you prayed for him to die in his sleep?'

Veronica snapped, 'Sam, let it be. Don't judge her. It's not like she killed him. She did the best she could. To err is human, Sam.'

Sam closed her eyes and took a deep sigh. She then looked at her mom and said, 'I am so thankful for you, mom. If only everyone could be like you. I owe everything in my life to you. You are the greatest mother ever. I love you, mom.'

Mrs. Joseph hugged Sam again and cried, even more, this time.

'Samantha Madam, I wish I was as lucky as you. I wish my father had died along with my mother, and maybe I would have ended up, with someone like your mother instead. Then my life would have been a fairytale too,' Pinky said with tears in her eyes.

Veronica shook her head and said, 'It's the ecosystem. Big fish eat small fish. That's the rule.'

'I'm sorry, my dear. I will help you to find your destiny now. You are my orphanage sister in a strange way. I guess, not everyone is lucky enough to be born or brought up by the right set of parents.' Sam vowed to play a reciprocal, complementary role henceforth while she looked at her mother with eyes full of tears of gratitude.

In the heat of the moment, Mrs. Joseph said, 'I have to confess. My guilty conscience is killing me.'

All three girls were looking at Mrs. Joseph with a whetted curiosity. They had no idea that they were about to hear the dramatic story from the horse's mouth.

She began, 'Just before I adopted Sam at the orphanage, Ratan Singh came to us running one day and said that he was hoping for us to adopt the 3-year old Pinky. He wanted to give her up because he was aware of his poor finances. Also, Pinky's mother had died, and Ratan Singh had no other family to bank upon. Worse of all, he had been diagnosed with the initiation of liver cirrhosis.' Mrs. Joseph held Sam's hands now as she was trembling.

'And you picked me instead because . . .?' Sam asked her mother, putting her on the spot with a stern stare that said, *Please don't let your answer be the horror that would leave me doomed and make everything about my life meaningless. Please don't say that you picked me over Pinky because of her birthmark. Please don't make the tables turn. Please don't take my amazing mother away from me and replace her with a sanctimonious evil witch.*

Mrs. Joseph kissed Sam on the forehead and let her tears drop before taking the cat out of the bag: 'I will cut the goddess act and get straight to my culpable and sadistic self now. I can't tell you how much I hate myself today, but the truth is that I picked you because you were beautiful and Pinky had a birthmark on her face.'

The Truth of a Myth

Kabhi Ram Banke, Kabhi Shyam Banke, Chale Aana, echoed the melody of a devotional song.

It was a typical evening in the *Santoshi Mata Mandir*—one of the countless local Hindu temples in the country. A group of a hundred females adorning sarees of various colours and textures were singing and dancing to *God* at their loudest. If that wasn't noisy enough, they were also playing traditional instruments including the dholak with the customary spoon-thumping and hand cymbals. The temple walls resonated as it happens in case of a boisterous band of amateur musicians playing at a high school open mic day, trying their luck. The religious ladies weren't bothered about fine-tuning the percussion. They were having the time of their lives dancing to the lively tunes of their *bhajans*. It was their meditation. Their *nirvana*!

These women devoted themselves to God and prayed regularly. They took pride in their spirituality. Sudha Aggarwal was one of them; although she was one of a kind. She was a zealot when it came to religion and God-fearing notions, but with an additional problem—Sudha's brain was wired with blind faith.

Sudha was a step ahead of her peers when it came to traditions, rituals and age-old superstitions. For instance, she never walked the street if a black cat had crossed it—because it was a bad omen. She would never sweep her house at night or wash her hair on a Thursday or Saturday. She never let footwear stay upside down, apparently to 'avoid quarrels'. She would always put *kaala teeka* behind children's ears in the family. She believed in *buri nazar* and *buri kismet*. She avoided being eye to eye with a *lower caste* person. She trusted intricate notions more than she honoured good karma. And the cherry on top was Sudha's earnest belief in Murphy's first law of nature: *anything that can go wrong will go wrong* unless you can turn it around with a few *totkas* (tricks).

Sadly, there were many like Sudha, people whose lives and deaths were consumed with traditional beliefs. Though religion teaches one to be kind, such people were eager to put anyone's life at stake to satisfy their mythical faith. Their superstitions defined their lives.

The *Kirtan* and chanting ended after 3 hours. A bunch of people gathered around the *prasad* distribution table just outside the temple entrance. Sudha was hosting *Langar* just like every other week.

Sudha was dressed in a pure silk maroon-coloured saree with a golden border and was sporting a pure *Kundan* necklace with matching earrings. Her wrists were loaded with a dozen bangles on the left side and a *Kundan* bracelet on the right, along with three gold rings on each hand. She completed her look with a red circular *bindi* on her forehead and a vertical red line of vermilion or *sindoor* in her midline hair partition.

She sneaked into the temple to meet the priest, leaving her *Prasad* table reign behind.

'*Panditji*, why are you taking so long to answer? Is everything ok with the *Kundli*?'

'I don't know how to tell you this, but this girl that you are so desperate to make your daughter-in-law is *bad luck*. Her *Saturn* is powerful and can be the cause of a disastrous life for the next seven years. She will make your son miserable.'

'But I liked this girl for Sunil. She is beautiful and homely. Her family is very religious. Is there no way out? Please work the magic of your superpowers.'

'I would have if I could. No last straw.'

'Tsk Tsk. It is such a shame the family never disclosed it. As if I wouldn't have dug every little grain of dirt on her. I can't risk it. Thank you, *Panditji*. Here's a *Dakshina.*' Sudha slid a sum of Rs 5100 into the priest's palm.

Sudha had two sons—Sunil who was 24 years old and Anil who was 20. Her husband, Ram Chand Aggarwal, ran a jewellery store, which was quite successful. Sunil was affiliated to the store, and Anil was all set to follow his brother's footsteps soon enough. The store was under *God's blessings* that was made sure by Mrs. Aggarwal's reassurance by a repetition of *havans* and *poojas* seeking prosperity. She reminded *God* now and then to keep her family on top through her devotion.

Mrs. Aggarwal was always following everything she was supposed to follow and was avoiding everything she was supposed to prevent. She didn't let any blasphemy or shadow of lousy luck come near her family. She was prepared for everything beforehand. She had weapons to fight all devils in the form of sacred threads and *kaala teeka*.

Sunil was all set to get married to someone who was from the same caste, who was wealthy enough and on top of all who had a non-controversial *Kundli.* The shocking truth came out when the family started having talks about meeting a prospective girl who was approved beforehand by astrology and by Sudha's mentor and well-wisher priest—*Panditji*.

'Mummy, I can't meet anyone. I am dating a girl for the last two years, and I want to marry her.'

'Please give me her details—her family background, her household skills, her photograph and most importantly, her *Kundli*. I will talk to *Panditji* and let you know by to-night.'

'No. She doesn't have any of those. She lives with her mother in a small apartment close by and works as a teacher in a local school. Since she is a Christian, she has no *Kundli*.'

'Are you serious, Sunil? This can *never* happen. She clearly has a lot of baggage. She isn't a Hindu, either!' Sudha envisioned her son's fiasco in the love of his life.

'But she is the best person I know. I think you are going to love her if you just gave her a chance. Would you please meet her? For me? Don't jeopardize my relationship over some lame belief.'

'You know my answer, Sunil. Stop beating about the bush. We are going to meet the girl that *Panditji* has approved for you. No further discussions.' Sudha reinforced.

Sunil let go of his feelings and did as asked. He got married to the girl of his mother's choice. His wife, Aarti, had a warm personality and settled well into the family. She built an equation with everyone at home. Sudha was happy and proud of her choice. Two years later; Sunil and Aarti had a son. He was named Harsh by the grace of *Panditji*. But as the events unfolded, Harsh had some issues.

'*Panditji*, what's wrong with Harsh's *Kundli*?'

'It is not a big deal. He is fixable. You just need to do a *havan* every week at the temple until he turns nine. That should suffice for the demon out of Harsh's life.'

'No problem at all. Reserve the temple every week for it, followed by a lavish feast every time. This is my grandson's future. I cannot take any chances.'

The series of *havans* began like an epic TV series and continued streaming every week at the temple. Sudha never skipped and dragged Aarti and Harsh along. Three years passed by, and nothing changed. Mr. Aggarwal and Sunil had been working and prospering at the jewellery store, which now had three branches. Anil, on the other hand, was completing a master's degree in Engineering in another city.

Mr. Aggarwal built a mansion for his family with Italian architecture and decor. He moved heaven and earth to include every luxury. It was a dream house. All family members were thrilled to celebrate the occasion. The Aggarwal family hosted a grand Housewarming Party with an avalanche of guests. Anil was back for the event from his hostel.

Aarti went to the stage and gave a brief speech.

'We are lucky to have the world's best parents. My father-in-law has given us every comfort in life, and we all are thankful. But, my mother-in-law had a major role to play. She has warded off all evils on the way and made everything possible. She is the lucky charm for our family. We are grateful to have her.'

Sudha wiped off her tears after listening to her. A few minutes later, Anil came to her, with a girl next to him.

'She is Aditi. We have been seeing each other for a year now, and I just wanted her to meet you.'

'Oh. Welcome, Aditi. How are you?'

'I am fine, thank you, aunty. It's great to be here. You have such an amazing house.'

'Yes. His father is very passionate about it. What about your family, though?'

'My family is not very different from this. My father, Ramesh Gupta, is the owner of Shanti Towers.'

'Of course. Who doesn't know about Shanti Towers? Your father is a great man. How did you meet her, Anil?'

'Well, we are studying together. We are in the same engineering college.'

'What? What are you studying, Aditi?'

'I am doing masters too. Just like your son.'

'Okay. But Anil is finishing up soon. It's so great that you like studying too.'

'Yes. I do. I am already talking to a couple of companies here for a job. You see, I am also finishing in six months.'

'Great meeting you, Aditi.'

After the party was over, Sudha started spiralling. She wanted a girl from the same caste and good family background for Anil. However, Aditi was ambitious too. She didn't know if Aditi would be ok with following religious rituals. She knocked on Anil's bedroom door.

'It's late. Are you alright, Mummy?'

'I want Aditi's details. I have to show her *Kundli* to *Panditji*.'

'She doesn't have a *Kundli*. Not everyone believes in astrology. It is contentious.'

'You know I can't let you marry her until your *Kundlis* match.'

'I don't care about the *Kundli*. I am going to marry Aditi. I am done getting manipulated.'

'I won't be happy. Please, son. Even if you don't believe in these things, you need to respect me. If she doesn't have a *Kundli*, get me her date and time of birth. Plus, a few other tiny details.'

'That is being pedantic and nosy. I am not going to ask her that. Her family is not as conservative. It's my plight that you believe in such stuff. I will end up making a fool of myself.'

'Do it. It's an order.'

'Mummy, is it not possible for you to look past all this? Aditi is perfect. She has a distinguished family background and belongs to our caste. Moreover, you can't undermine her accomplishments. She is a scholar who is destined to make a leading engineer soon. She is better than anyone I know. I know it will all go out of the window if her stupid *Kundli* isn't up to your standards.'

'I do not deny her worth. She could become the President of India one day. But that worth is nothing if her stars don't match yours for her to be your future wife.'

Anil gave up after hearing this. He helplessly agreed and got the details. Aditi seemed pretty understanding and docile about the entire thing.

'Aditi is *Manglik*. Anil will die if he gets married to her.'

'No *Panditji*. This is not possible. Are you sure?'

'Absolutely sure. She is a bad omen for him.'

'But he won't agree. He wasn't even ready to try.'

'You have to get him out of this. He will die unless. . . .'

'Unless what, *Panditji*?'

'Unless she passes on her marital omen to someone else or, something else.'

'Like a tree?'

'Yes. A specific kind of tree.'

'Great. You are great, *Panditji.* You can solve all the problems. Here's your *Dakshina* of Rs. 11000. Thank you very much. I will be back with Aditi.'

Sudha disclosed the news to Anil who at once disagreed. The entire family was present except Aarti and her son who were at Aarti's parents' house for a couple of days to visit. That's when the mother and son started arguing at the dining table.

'Not going to happen. Why don't you just start a business of correcting people's destiny with your maledictions?' Anil was flustered with her mother's beliefs.

'No, son. I can't risk your life. If you think that she is too good to follow our culture and rituals, then I will not agree to your marriage.'

'I will not back off as Sunil did in the past. I will marry Aditi. Whether you like it or not. You and your superman *Panditji* cannot change my mind.'

'I think we should consider Aditi,' exclaimed Mr. Aggarwal (Sudha's husband). Sudha shook her head in disapproval while staring at her husband.

'I beg you, Anil. Please don't ruin your future. A wife's fate can affect the husband's very strongly,' Sudha said to Anil while holding his hand.

'Yeah! Like your and Papa's?'

'Yes. Think about it, even about your brother and Aarti. Imagine if he had married that Christian girl, he would be doomed.'

'What are you talking about? Who is the Christian girl?' asked Mr. Aggarwal.

'Papa, I had an affair before getting married to Aarti. She was a Christian, and hence mummy disapproved,' Sunil jumped in.

'How come I never heard of it?' The father was shocked.

'It all worked out for the best, Papa. I have no regrets. I am delighted to have Aarti,' Sunil reassured.

'Lucky for you, brother. I am never going to be happy without Aditi. I love her,' Anil inferred.

'Why don't you ask her to do what *Panditji* said? If she loves you too, I don't see it being a problem. Given she might kill you otherwise—her *Kundli* is culpable.' Sudha was all set to bear down on the issue.

'To hell with your *Panditji*. He is a vulture who feasts upon other people's ignorance and idiosyncrasies. I am not so petty. I won't live if Aditi isn't there to share my life with me. I will not ask her to marry a tree or a dog for that matter. It's demeaning,' Anil was exasperated.

'Son, you will never be able to make me say yes to this. I can't put your life in danger,' Sudha wiped her tears while talking.

'Stop being so finicky. Sunil missed his chance, and I can't tell you how sorry I am for not intervening before. I wish I had known what was going on. Nevertheless, it is time to let the cat out of the bag. I have something to tell you, Sudha,' said Mr. Aggarwal in a profoundly intense tone.

'We have been married for almost 30 years now. I am still alive, and you have been nothing but lucky for me,' he continued.

'Yes and that's because your mother got our *Kundlis* tested before marriage and they were a perfect match. We had a love marriage too, but the stars approved it. Our fates matched and *Panditji's* father did it for us at that time. We are together because of our *Kundlis* and not just because we love each other. I would have been devastated if the *Kundlis* didn't match and we didn't get married. I might have killed myself,' Sudha broke down with her head on the dining table.

'Our *Kundlis* were never a match, Sudha. My mother was from an orthodox background but she was extremely open-minded. She passed away within a couple of months after our marriage and so you couldn't see the real her. She knew she was terminally ill, and I was her only child,' Sudha's husband was opening some long lost tales.

'So?'

'So, she just couldn't leave me behind with a life full of sadness. She knew that only you could make me happy. She always mocked superstitions and called them tiresome and senseless. She wanted to leave me happy after she died. However, reaching an impasse on something of sorts with the rest of the family in those times was an impossible task. So she faked. She lied to everyone but me.'

'What?' Sudha began to feel pins and needles on herself.

'Sudha, you were a *Manglik,* just like Aditi. You were even worse. Your dearest *Panditji's* father was running the temple at that time and he came to our house to test the *Kundlis*. I was there the entire time. He said that even a tree or a dog couldn't take your evil away and your husband was destined to die. Nothing could change it. My mother bribed the old *Panditji* to keep his mouth shut,' Mr. Aggarwal confessed.

'So, that means that my mother-in-law lied to everybody about our *Kundli* matching and put your life in danger, just to make you happy? It is relentless. I can't do that to my son,' Sudha ranted.

'You already did it to Sunil. I never paid any attention to it because all I thought you were doing was praying. I was ignorant and I regret it whole-heartedly. We are just fortunate that Sunil and Aarti are happy together,' he added.

'They were made for each other,' Sudha said wholeheartedly.

Sunil got overly worked up. It had taken him a while to get comfortable with Aarti after marrying her because of the abrupt end to his previous relationship. He had to put in a lot of effort to build an equation with his wife. Sunil had disclosed everything to Aarti within the first month of their marriage. He considered himself lucky as Aarti was a considerate human being who always stood committed to him. They had taken their time to adjust but luckily ended up liking each other.

After the birth of their child, Sudha was again pushing Sunil to blindly follow *Panditji* to clear up the baby Harsh's destiny. Sunil was never ready for it. But Aarti had convinced him by saying that it would make his mother extremely delighted. Moreover, she volunteered to do it with her every time. Aarti had even pushed her limits and insisted on giving a speech on stage at the housewarming party. She did everything in her power to make Sudha happy.

Sunil kept up his side of the marriage by leaving no stone unturned. He cared for Aarti more than anyone. He expressed his love from time to time. He took into account all small and big things that Aarti liked, such as flowers, mangoes, green sarees, Thai food, bright curtains, novels, and post-dinner long walks. He never shied away from telling her how unexpectedly and yet how naturally he had fallen in love with her and Aarti reciprocated it on every front.

Hence, Sunil couldn't stand the thought of his mother crediting fate and mythology for their love.

He agitatedly remarked, 'Probably. But are you giving all the credit to *Panditji*? Is that why all the happily married couples are happily married? Because of *Kundli* matching? Are you still not able to see the authenticity of these myths? Do I have to spell it out for you? You do realize that your husband is still alive and couldn't have had a better life?'

Sudha was at a loss of words. Her entire life was turning up a lie. She felt like holding sand of beliefs that she wanted to keep saving, but it was slipping off. She was bewildered and couldn't understand the puzzle of life. She still couldn't believe it all.

'Goodness me! It's astounding. If I had *Kundli dosh*, why are you not dead?' she remarked, questioning her husband.

'Because I have a great wife. Just as Anil will have one, I killed two birds with one stone, my dear. Your *Kundli dosh* didn't stop me from being invincible,' said Sudha's husband.

Sudha swallowed her agony. She fumbled with the bite of *roti* in her hand for a while and had a glass of water. She thought about Aarti and how incredibly nice she had been to the family. She even remembered how she had cried after the speech Aarti gave at the housewarming and had thought to herself: *I should be thankful to Panditji for giving me Aarti.*

She then realized how unrealistic and cumbersome the *havans* had been. How Sudha had not paid enough attention to the shlokas anymore and how disinterested Harsh had been during each one of them. She remembered Aarti trying her best to keep Harsh sit down for the entire duration every time. Was Aarti just a good person and her stars had nothing to do with it? Was her husband lying about her *Kundli dosh*?

'I need your phone, Anil.'

Anil handed over his phone to Sudha with a scared look. He had no idea who his mother was going to call. Sudha dialled a number and waited for the person on the other end to answer.

'Hello, Mrs. Sharma. I have a rather odd question. When your son died last month within two months of getting married, it made me think. Did you not get the *Kundlis* tested?'

She hung up the phone after she got her answer from Mrs. Sharma and dialled another number from Anil's contact list. The person answered.

'Hello, Aditi. This is Anil's mother. I have learnt my lesson. A *Manglik* girl's husband is still alive after thirty years of marriage and on the contrary, a marriage that took place after a perfect *Kundli* match ended up in the death of the husband. Also, I learnt that happy marriages are made out of compatibility, commitment and choice more than *kismet*. So on that note, will you please marry my son?'

Aditi answered, 'Yes, Aunty. Can't wait.'

Superwoman

It was Wednesday mid-morning in Delhi. Soon after the abandonment of the crowded city by professionals who had now taken refuge in their respective workplaces, the peak rush hour was over. The city had finally become livable, just like every other weekday afternoon. The Delhi Metro became a bit more breathable as the number of sweaty armpits it had to endure everyday reduced dramatically.

Diya was sitting next to a random woman on the last seat of the *ladies* compartment. The following connecting metro rail compartment was a general one.

Diya was a talker. She began a conversation with the woman. 'It is impossible to travel in the metro before eleven a.m. The crowd is like a circus.'

'I agree! The high tide of morning rush crushes me so bad that I feel I'm developing wrinkles and creases all over my body. I usually travel earlier for work, but today was an exception because my maid came late,' replied the woman.

'Wow! Maids are such a problem! I always wonder how people manage them. Your entire day depends on whether or not they come to your house on time.'

'*Poochho Mat* (Don't ask)! I change maids every couple of months, but nobody seems to be decent enough. The frequent change wreaks havoc in our lives.'

'Poor you. I understand that maids have their problems, but I'm sure we all can meet midway.'

'Yeah. I do try to do that.' The woman giggled sarcastically.

Just then, a man began talking on his mobile phone with his pitch so loud that people near and far could hear the conversation.

'Her father is so stubborn. He won't agree to our marriage at all. He said it to my face. He thinks that I am a gangster. He said that he doesn't care if our *Papaji* is an MLA. He is not going to let Nidhi marry me. What a moron! Looks like he has completely lost his mind. *Wo jaanta nahi main kaun hoon!* (He doesn't know who he is dealing with!) I want Nidhi—and I will get her. By hook or by crook. I will ask her to come and marry me regardless of whether her father approves or not. I don't think I can get a girl better than Nidhi. She is my best one; *yet*.'

Diya was smiling. She said to the woman, 'He thinks big of the girl. But marrying without parents' approval is almost impossible for a girl. I wish we had the same kind of freedom as boys.'

'You know what I think? This boy is biting off more than he can chew. This girl seems too good for him. He sounds dubious,' the woman said to Diya.

The man continued, '*Bhai,* you are right. That man has made me very angry. He is trying to emasculate me. He thinks Nidhi is too good for me. I have to do something. Who does he think he is? I will teach him a lesson. If Nidhi comes to me, I will get married to her and then the very next day—I'll disappear.'

Diya became a bundle of nerves listening to this vicious plan. 'What is this man talking about? Outrageous! I thought he was fond of this girl Nidhi. On the contrary, he is planning to ruin her life.'

The situation called for a drastic measure. It was time to exercise her secret superpower. Diya confirmed the time in her digital wristwatch as 11:46:14. She closed her eyes and took a deep breath. Time stopped in all wristwatches and mobile phones, as it were. Everything and everyone froze at that moment in the city—the Delhi metro, the cars on the street including the one transferring the prime minister to the parliament and everything else stood motionless. The only person barring the stillness was Diya. It looked like a graphic scene from a sci-fi movie.

Diya got off from her seat and went up to the guy talking on the phone who was still holding the phone up against his ear. She took away the phone and left his hand hanging. She then went through the man's Facebook, where she noticed how Nidhi had tagged him in her pictures almost every day. Nidhi's relationship status was: 'in a relationship with Ankur', the train guy himself. Ankur's Facebook profile, on the other hand, had nothing about Nidhi. She then kissed the guy and took a picture of herself from the back, doing so with the guy's phone and boom! She posted it on his Facebook wall saying: 'My new girl!'

Diya returned to her seat and rechecked the time in her wristwatch as 11:46:14. She closed her eyes again and brought everything back to normal with her wristwatch getting back to running time to 11:46:15, 11:46:16. . . .

The man's phone began to ring, and he was suddenly heard saying, 'No way! I'm sorry. . . . My picture? Kissing a girl? I don't know how it happened. . . But . . . I only love you. . . . Your father is stupid . . . you can't be so hostile to me. Nidhi, please trust me. . . No . . . Don't . . . Nidhi . . . Nidhi . . . Please . . . Hello . . . Hello. . .' Nidhi had hung up the phone.

The woman next to her said, 'That water changed tides faster than I could imagine. The predator became the prey!' Diya smiled with delight, waved the woman goodbye and got off at the next stop to find another victim on another train ride.

After some time, Diya boarded the Delhi Metro train again in the ladies-only compartment. The six p.m. rush hour had started, and people started pushing each other and climbing on top of each other's feet to get a tiny space to land inside the train after work. In an overly crowded train, just when the train was about to reach *Rajiv Chowk* metro station, a commotion began.

'My phone! It has been stolen. I had it right here in my jeans pocket. Who took it? Please, Please, Please—give it back. I can't afford to lose my phone. Please!'

A girl started yelling and crying. She seemed helpless. Diya was able to hear her but couldn't see her face because of the crowd.

'I am going to complain at the next stop. Right away. Last chance to return my phone or else I am getting off and going straight to the security and to the police.'

The girl sounded helpless and distressed.

'I was about to receive an urgent phone call. Please give me my phone back.'

She pleaded further. Nobody came forward to return her phone.

The girl got off at Rajiv Chowk and so did Diya along with a hundred other people. Diya followed the girl from behind, hoping to help her. She reached her hand on the girl's head and closed her eyes for five seconds and stopped the time at 18:11:29 in her wristwatch.

Let's see if her phone was stolen. It might still be with her.

Diya saw that the mobile phone was not stolen, but it had just died because of a no-battery charge inside the girl's bag. Diya then turned back to the girl and saw a tear-drop hanging halfway down her cheek, hanging onto her skin, paused in time with Diya's superpower. Diya took a deep breath with frustration and then flicked away the tear-drop.

Teenagers are stupid. So dramatic.

Diya thought to herself before reaching for the phone inside the bag. She magically charged it and switched it on. She went through the girl's texts and WhatsApp chat exchanges.

'I am pretty sure you will get it. I have no doubts.'

'Yes, Danny. I'm very hopeful. Your aunty is the boss. My future is in her hands.'

'It's ok to be nervous. Just take a deep breath. I promised you I'd talk to her.'

'But have you kept your promise? I kept mine! You had fun with my pictures.'

'I will. You will get the part, Alyson. But you need to send some more.'

'Really? To hell with your aunt and hell with the part. I'm not doing it. I liked you, and I thought you liked me back when I sent you my sensual photos last week. Then I

found out about your girlfriend. You keep your part and leave me alone. Besides, why don't you ask your girlfriend for her pictures?'

'Girlfriend? And what fun will that be? I might love her. But your body is a treat for sore eyes. My girlfriend is great. But she is not as pretty as you.'

'Please don't be so insensitive. Don't you have a heart?'

'Heart is for gays. I'm a man.'

'STFU! Gay men are men too.'

'Nope! They are gays, and I don't support gays. It's an abomination.'

'You're a moron.'

'Do you want that role or not? And you might have forgotten that even though I asked you to delete those pictures from your phone, I've still got them. I will send them to all my friends to enjoy it.'

'Please! Ok! I will send you more.'

'You have one hour.'

Diya jumped out of her skin on reading the chat exchange. The one hour was about to finish in 20 minutes as per the timing of messages. She had to get the hapless girl out of this mess and also teach this blackmailer a lesson.

She thought of a quick solution. First, Diya worked her superpowers, and through Alyson's phone, she touched Danny's WhatsApp profile picture and was straightaway able to access his phone wholly. She deleted all of Alyson's images from Danny's photo albums and online storage accounts. Then, to humiliate him, she magically added a boy's back of the head and neck into Danny's profile picture and changed the background to LGBTQ rainbow. Diya returned to Alyson's side and turned everything back to normal. She then handed over the phone back to Alyson and told her, 'you dropped it inside the train.'

Alyson smiled and thanked Diya before going through her phone to check on Danny. She couldn't believe herself. 'How did Danny declare himself as gay?' Alyson asked herself.

'Maybe he had a girlfriend just for pretence until he dared to come out.' Diya said.

'How did you? Did you go through my phone?' Alyson asked Diya.

'Yeah! Sorry. Notifications on the screen. But the moral of the story is that you never send your objectionable pictures to any guy. Even if you are attracted to him, it's a miracle you are out of the mess.' Diya told Alyson before leaving Alyson's sight who was now alarmed about the mysterious encounter, but at the same time, relieved. Diya had killed two birds with one stone. She mitigated Alyson's cyber assault, and she rescued Danny's girlfriend from a cheating chauvinist boyfriend. And then, Diya walked away, leaving Alyson to enjoy a guilt-free life.

The next morning came. Diya appeared at the metro station at 05:29:00 and looked around for her next humanitarian adventure. The watch on Diya's hand was ticking, and the time now was 05:31:00. Diya froze at the moment. She didn't know what was happening to her. All she could see now was the big digital display TV screen on the platform. The small number of people at the station at that time were all glued to it. It showed a group of young girls outside the *Tihar Jail* echoing a countdown . . . 10, 9, 8 . . . 3, 2, 1. *Breaking News: Four rape convicts of the rape case that happened seven years ago, hanged to death a minute back at Tihar Jail in Delhi.* Diya immediately teleported herself back to the monstrous rape site.

Diya saw herself taking a bus back home after a movie date with her boyfriend. Diya saw five men slut-shaming her for being out at that hour with a boy, which was out of bounds for a patriarchal cultural mindset. The men who had been born and brought up to believe that women are beneath men; such men believe that women are like flowers which are soft and weak, while men are the thorns on those flowers which are stiff and robust. Thorns protect their flowers. Additionally, if a flower were to decide to slip away from their *traditional* branch and end up in a gutter, it ruins itself. Whereas, if it lands in a temple, it is placed next to god. Metaphorically, gutter is the modern outage of a woman who wears western clothes and goes out on dates; and this temple is formed by patriarchal norms. That's all they had seen throughout their poor and ignored childhoods, and that's all they had done during their fucked up youths. They belonged to the section of society which did not know any better.

Then, these men went for the heinous outage and carried out a barbaric crime on Diya—a crime positioned lower than death for a woman in the hierarchy of catastrophes. A crime that outcasts a woman who discloses her suffering. A crime that haunts the victim at every juncture—while reporting to the police, while getting a medical examination and then every night for the rest of her life while she tries to sleep. That is—if she survives. A crime that goes unreported because of all the reasons above in 9 out of 10 cases. A crime that brands a woman as *been raped* before it brands the person doing it, a *rapist*. A crime that makes a woman pray that she was either born a boy or not at all. The 5 travellers and the driver of the bus had gang-raped Diya in a moving bus.

Diya stood next to the crime in action in her past life. She saw herself lying helpless in a pool of blood and screaming on the top of her lungs. But this time there was no superhero or saviour. She saw herself bleed and suffer while 5 men took turns to rape her whilst amusing themselves and mocking at the unfortunate victim. To add to her horror, she saw them tormenting her soul-less body further by penetrating an iron rod into her vagina and her rectum, repeating the *in and out thrust* with the serrated end of the rod inside her. She wanted to look away from herself. The demons showed no shame and threw her almost lifeless bleeding naked body out of the bus, to die of pain, shame and misery. She was perished.

Diya had no memory of her past until that moment. Diya saw herself die days later of the appalling injuries.

A few moments after her death, Diya woke up inside the Delhi Metro train in her afterlife, not remembering anything about her past existence. She had no idea about who she was or where she was going. She just felt extremely powerful sitting in her seat. Her senses were heightened and her judgement felt accurate. She looked around and could see and hear vulnerable women magically highlighted. She was gifted with superpowers to help others walk out of their miserable cocoons.

Her instincts could sense women who were belittled or ignored by society and were almost in a state of having their lives ruined. Some of these women were expected to *go with the flow*. Diya felt outraged only wishing to bring hell to the demons of this horrendous society who objectify women, treat them like sex-slaves and dump them into soil and garbage. She had been fighting to convert molesting predators into preys of femme fatalist defence. But it has been a one-sided battle until society eradicates its pseudo-masculinity. And Diya had been fighting it for seven years now. One of the rapists had said in a special interview that if Diya's rapists got a death penalty after her police complaint, which was made before her death, other rapists would never leave a victim alive to talk later. All such gnawing thoughts seemed to creep through Diya's ear, all the way to her brain. She felt she died again. She didn't know if she should have reported the crime and put other women in danger of getting killed before complaining.

Diya finally realized the purpose of her existence as a superwoman messiah in the afterlife. She knew now that since Delhi's heartbeat was the Delhi metro, she was able to find a woman suffering every hour. When she came back from her gut-wrenching memories to the present on the Delhi metro station, standing in front of the television, looking at that piece of news, she said to herself, 'I will make sure there are no more superwomen like myself. Even if I'm the only one doing it.'

Then, she heard another interview. The students counting seconds before the hanging of Diya's rapists happened were on TV. The interviewer asked them if they had seen any change regarding the objectification of women after the conviction? One of the girls answered, 'The system and mentality of molesters might not have changed, but I have changed after that girl (Diya) went through such pain. I'm in the zero-tolerance zone now. I will not tolerate any more affliction.'

Those Kinds of Girls

Tarun was sitting on the top floor of the Starbucks outlet at Block A, CP, Delhi; thinking about a caption to post on to his cappuccino picture on Instagram.

'Is this table taken?'

A girl asked Tarun, pointing at the table next to him. Tarun shook his head in negative and the girl sat down. This was the very first time Tarun looked at her.

She may have been the prettiest girl Tarun had seen. She sported a black *Anarkali kurta* with mesmerizing hand-woven embroidery done with multicoloured threads on the borders of her 3/4th-arm-length sleeves, the neckline and the perimeter of the extra-flared *kurta.* The midline of the kurta had handloom buttons with the very purpose of making the outfit look even more eye-catching. The black *churidar* underneath was adding perfect balance and the breathtaking handloom dupatta, a multicoloured tie-and-dye masterpiece complementing the entire attire along with the black *jooti* with bright blue polka dots made an extravagant combination.

Tarun moved over to look at the girl's face, one that had flawless wheatish complexion. The adornments on this girl were a feast for the eyes. Her innocent looking face with minimal make-up around her cheeks and her nose, nude lipstick and the traces of dark black kohl around her eyes followed their contour perfectly and gave the eyes a sultry look. Tarun also noticed the silver *jhumkas* that were approximately a couple of inches long and a nose-ring that not only added character to the face but also seemed to be talking to Tarun—*don't look away. I am beautiful.*

Tarun smiled and tried to look away before his stare became obvious enough bordering a typical creep who has the superpower to see through girls' clothes. He quickly came back to his Instagram.

Then, after a minute or so, he heard the girl crying. He looked up and saw her trying to wipe her tears neatly without damaging her *kajal.* It must have been water-proof. She then tried to wipe the water dripping from her nose as she continued crying. She ended up taking her nose-ring off to be able to wipe off the snot properly. She kept looking at her phone while the sobbing continued.

Tarun tried to control his urge to talk to the pretty girl because he wasn't very confident when it came to breaking the ice with people. He wanted to address the girl—*hey pretty thing! I will rescue you from all evils. I will make you happy. I will ruin whoever has tried to destroy your gorgeous nose-ring.*

'Excuse me, ma'am. Ummmm . . . Are you alright? Can I help you?'

'Leave me alone. I am dealing with something.'

'Ok. Just trying to help.'

'Thanks.'

Tarun tried to play aloof afterwards and continued drinking his coffee. After another five minutes, the crying intensified. Other people sitting around started looking at the girl. Tarun felt obliged now.

'Look, if you could just tell me how can I help you?'

'You are not my knight in shining armour. And I am definitely not a damsel in distress.'

'You kind of are in some sort of distress. I'm not your knight, but I am a human being. I can't sit next to you and pretend not to hear you cry. '

'Look! Thanks for your concern. But it's a private matter. You can't do anything. Nobody can!'

'I respect your privacy. But the way you are crying in public is alarming. So, please tell me what's wrong? By the way, my name is Tarun . . . just trust me.'

The girl looked around and saw many eyes staring at her. She tried to avoid eye contact with anyone but Tarun. She leaned pretty close to him. Tarun thought—*Isn't she too close? Is she doing it on purpose? Is it a gimmick?*

She then whispered into his ear after a couple of sobs, 'I'm Neha. I failed my university final exams. Just got my result. I feel so stupid. I couldn't even become a graduate. My father's going to get me married to a good-for-nothing loser. I am a mess and . . . I'm doomed.'

'I empathize with you. But you just admitted that you failed graduation and you are calling another person a loser. . . .'

'That's perhaps because you don't know that I am an artist. My father doesn't care about my passion. He forced me to graduate in History when I don't even know the difference between *Diwan-i-Aam* and *Diwan-i-Khas.*'

'Doesn't matter what he thinks. I don't understand the logic of him getting you married.'

'You can't. Gosh! I wish I were a boy.'

'If you were a boy, would your father value your art?'

'Value? He would be so proud of it. He wouldn't think of getting rid of me by getting me married at this age. I am just 22.'

'I'm sorry, but we can think of a solution.'

'There is no solution. God! I don't know what to do.'

Tarun thought to himself—*Neha, why am I so attracted to you? I just can't take my eyes off you.*

After a brief pause and a sigh, Tarun decided—*I am going to help her. It is my duty as a human being.*

'Neha, what kind of art do you create? I mean, do you have any recognition? Big or small? How about social media? Do you have any followers?'

'I am not on social media. My father didn't allow me.'

'Well, you can reach millions on social media.'

'You don't understand. I never go against my father's wishes. I always follow what he says. Always!'

'Look, with all due respect, that makes no sense to me. You are ruining your life. Being a father doesn't mean he can direct your life for you. This is 2020! Are you serious in telling me that even today parents can stop their children, who are—in fact, not children anymore—from having a social media account?'

'*Arre haan*. It is true. I respect my father a lot.'

'Neha. You sound like a child to me now. Make a social media account and don't tell your father about it. Use a disguised name and add a collage of your paintings. Simple!'

'I can't do that. No girls in my family can. We are not *those kinds of girls*.'

'Ok . . . so go and become a wife at 22 and a mother at 24 and forget about your dreams. What do they call it . . . ahhhh . . . the path of least resistance!'

'Look, I don't need your judgement. I am not your typical Delhi girl who can do whatever she likes. I am from a small place in district Gorakhpur. I was born and brought up in a very conservative family. I wasn't even allowed to go to the playground after 6 or wear jeans for that matter. We moved to Delhi last year, and I took a transfer into Delhi University. I have been trained to obey. I don't know any better.'

Tarun couldn't believe himself after getting to know the real story behind an overly attractive girl who had just sat down next to him at a Starbucks.

Three years had elapsed. Neha sipped her coffee as she recalled her first meeting with Tarun—the love of her life, at the exact spot where she was sitting. Tarun was not just Neha's knight in shining armour. He was her loyal companion whom she was not allowed to marry because he belonged to a different *caste*.

Just then, Neha answered her mobile phone with no idea of what was coming her way.

'Sorry, Madam! I am calling regarding your husband—Pankaj.'

'What? But what exactly did he do?'

'Such a shame. Your husband is a pervert.'

'I know. But he is my husband. Nothing can change that. But why aren't you telling me what exactly happened? Actually . . . forget it. I will come right away.'

'*Arre* Madam, hold on. You can't do it for 24 hours.'

After hanging up the phone, Neha began to cry like she did when she met Tarun for the first time. She was loud. This time, a girl was sitting next to her. She was in her early twenties and was wearing relaxed fit—distressed denim pants and a fitted-feminine-flowery blouse which showed off her prominent collar bones. Her bare neck displayed a platinum neck chain. She was working in a pensive mode on her laptop and eating off small bites of the slice of tiramisu cake off her plate. She got startled by Neha's cry.

'Excuse me! Are you alright?'

'Please leave me alone . . . for God's sake.'

'Okay. But it seems like you could use some help. Here, take some water first. Calm down.'

Neha took a deep breath after sipping the water and said, 'Thanks for the water. But I think I am OK.'

'No problem. You take care. My name is Priya, and I feel that you shouldn't be stressing yourself up over anything in this condition. I wasn't planning on eavesdropping, but I happened to hear that your husband is in some kind of trouble.'

'But some things can't be helped, Priya. Pregnant or not. I was born unlucky. My name is Unlucky Neha.'

'How far are you? I mean with the pregnancy.'

'6 months,' answered a gruesome Neha.

'Hmmm! Are you sure I can't help you with anything?'

'Have you ever been molested? I mean . . . sexually?' Neha went straight for the kill.

'What?'

'Exactly. Girls who are born wearing a fairy dress and a princess crown, who can do whatever they want, who don't have to follow rulebooks, who can be with anyone they like and most importantly, who can become whatever they want to be!' Neha didn't realize how loud she was. Everyone around her heard everything.

'That's absurd. What a bold assumption! I don't want to help you anymore. You can go back to crying,' Priya responded with a sarcastic smile.

Neha broke into tears again. A group of two women and a teenage girl were sitting close-by. It seemed that they were a trio of mother, daughter and grand-daughter. They came over to Neha's table and tried to calm her down.

'Look, dear! Whatever it is, things do happen. You are carrying a child. Don't punish the child,' said the elderly woman.

All three pulled their chairs and sat down at Neha's table adjacent to Priya who seemed exasperated. Neha continued sobbing.

Priya wanted to be considerate. 'Neha, I am sorry for lashing out. You are obviously very upset, and I want to help you.'

'We all want to. My name is Nidhi, and this is my mother, Alka and my daughter Natasha. You can trust us. Tell us what's wrong?' asked Nidhi.

'Alright. But I don't want you all to judge me. Just leave if you think less of me after hearing the truth,' exclaimed Neha with a stern voice.

'My husband—Pankaj has been arrested for molesting a girl on the street. I am not sure what exactly happened, but they said it was outside her school. I need to find out and get him out of this.'

All the four females looked at each other, and after a short pause, Priya took Neha's hand and said, 'This isn't your fault. You should just care about yourself right now. If you think he is innocent, just find out a bit more'.

'Stop. I know he must have done it. It isn't the first time. It kind of is . . . my fault.'

'How!?' exclaimed Natasha.

'I was in love with a boy before marriage and never told my husband about him. He wriggled through my old stuff one day and then asked for a divorce. I begged him to stay, and he did. But he never loved me. I shouldn't have hidden my past from him. That's why he is like this.'

Everyone shook their heads, 'WHAT?'

Priya continued, 'Are you out of your mind, Neha? This is crazy as fuck!'

'Neha, do you think your husband has the right to assault other females because he doesn't love you and just because you didn't disclose your past love affair to him? Seriously?' Nidhi said with a disgusted look.

'Neha, no woman in this country is privileged enough to never-go-through a sexual assault in her lifetime. We have all had bitter experiences. But nothing can justify the behaviour of men who do it to us. The aftermath is daunting,' added Alka.

'I think you're wrong. Pankaj was devastated after he came to know about my past. He had a couple of panic attacks. It's not like he can control himself. But in this condition, he just hasn't been himself lately', Neha said with a feeling of self-pity.

Priya's eyes were wide open and about to pop out of her eye-sockets.

'See, you aren't even finding this odd. Sexual assault is not a question of whether . . . It's a question of how many times. Tell me how and why it can be justified? I want you to share your experiences.'

'Ok, Priya. But how is that going to get Pankaj out of jail? I can't have a child with no husband. I can't just leave him under the bus. I have to get Pankaj out,' Neha contemplated.

'Screw Pankaj and screw your attitude. Let's do this another way. We are five women of different age groups here. I am 100% sure that we all have something to share. I want to share my personal experience with you. We have all been in situations where men maltreated us. I am sure others also have similar stories. If you can convince me that supporting your husband is the right thing to do, I will accompany you to the police station and ask my boyfriend, who is a lawyer, to help your husband. Deal?' asked Priya.

Everyone nodded.

'Deal,' Neha shook hands with Priya.

Natasha took the lead and jumped into it right away. I'll start. Five years ago, I was 11 years old. I was in an all-girls' school. I had never spoken to an unrelated boy in my life . . . like, one-on-one. Then one day, I had to go to a friend's birthday party two streets down from my house; her brother's friend who was in college at the time was at the party. I couldn't understand why he never stopped smiling at me. We all began playing *dumb charades,* and we had to partner up. Guess what? He became my partner, and I thought that was just a coincidence. Honestly, I didn't know how to refuse because I was just really eager to team up with an older guy who I thought would be great at the game . . . you know, being older. He was extra sweet to me anyway. We played, and during the game, he tried to hug me as if I was his bestie. Can you believe that! I ran away after just four rounds of play. It was very apparent how uncomfortable I was. Then, this guy starts stalking me. He wandered outside my house day in and day out; he followed me to and fro my bus-stop; and if that wasn't enough, he came to the playground and stood there for the entire time I played with other kids. Then, he got my number from somewhere and started calling me non-stop. I was so scared! I tried to tell him off, but he insisted that I say *yes* to becoming his *girlfriend*. I was 11, and he was 20! I was so afflicted that I stopped doing anything normal. Then one day, mom found me crying in the bathroom, and I told her everything. Mom threatened the boy and his parents with police—so finally this was taken care of. But I still get nightmares. I still never feel totally safe outside my home,' Natasha wiped the emotion off her eyes as her mother held her.

There was an uncomfortable silence in the group.

Priya said, 'I'll go next. Five years ago, my friend and I attended a conference for a week, near the Delhi-UP border. We stayed in a hostel close to our venue in the middle of nowhere. There was absolutely nothing but farms around the three sides of our venue. There were barbed fences everywhere, but the security guards were only at the front gate. Although nobody could come inside the hostel, the farm was visible from our second-floor balcony. We had to walk to the venue and back. In these seven days, we were approached or almost groped thrice! Every time the target was a different body part. But that's not just it. One late evening after dinner, we decided to have tea on the common balcony facing the farm at the backside of the hostel.

Standing in front of us was this guy whom I immediately recognized from the groping incident. He came to the farm, and lustfully looked at us. He had a vicious smile and then . . . and then he pulled down his pants and started masturbating. It was scary. We ran back to our rooms and never went to the balcony again.' Priya had a look of horror after finishing her story.

Once more. An uncomfortable silence. A sense of inside rage.

Nidhi went next, 'My turn now. Even my mother and daughter haven't heard about this one, but it seems extremely important to tell them today. Almost 20 years ago, I used to travel to university every day on local buses. It was one such morning rush hour. Irrespective of how hot the weather and how sweaty the buses were, I would wear secure clothing to avoid giving anyone a glimpse of my bra strap or my panty border or my cleavage. That day, in particular, the bus broke down, and all passengers had to be accommodated in another bus. This new bus was now overcrowded. I began to feel dizzy and had a fainting sensation, so I took the liberty of taking off my neck scarf to wipe my sweat off. Looks like the man who was standing behind me got aroused. He had a lecherous look on his face. When he realized nobody was looking, he unzipped his pants and flashed his erect penis at me. Must've been the most disgusting thing I've ever seen. I couldn't think or say anything. I must've just frozen. I quickly got off the bus and took an auto-rickshaw to return home. I locked myself in my room and cried. I was terrified.' Nidhi looked at her daughter and her mother, who were both in tears.

The women embraced each other in solidarity; the rage was palpable, and so was the disgust.

Alka began her story next. 'I'm glad that Natasha is here because it is too much to handle for a little girl. She got her broken forearm plastered today and so didn't go to school. She is stressed. I didn't want her to know what grown-up girls have to face in this world. But I feel she should know what can happen and hence can protect herself better. My story is also terrifying. I was a schoolteacher all my life. When I started working, I was in my early twenties. There were no mobile phones back then. One way, I was walking back home from the bus-stop with my cousin who was 12 years old then and was a student in my school. It was around 3 p.m., and the sun was shining bright. I was wearing a saree with a sleeveless blouse, and my cousin was in her school uniform. We stopped at a hawker to drink a *kancha* lemon bottle each to beat the heat when suddenly, a car stopped very close to us and the man driving the empty car offered us a lift. I refused, but he insisted. I stopped talking, took my cousin's hand and started walking. It was a 15 minutes' walk back home, but there weren't many people around. After a couple of minutes of walking, I sighed with relief as I couldn't spot the car. Then, all of a sudden, I realized that the car was following us at a plodding speed. We were walking on the footpath next to the road. Then, the very next instant, the car came exactly by our side, and I saw a horrific act. The bastard was looking at us, and while driving his car extremely slowly with his left hand and with his right hand, he was . . . masturbating. I took my cousin's hand, who was too young to understand what was happening and ran away. It has been 35 years but I still distinctly remember the car and that man's face. This incident scarred me for life.' Alka took a heavy sigh while Nidhi hugged her.

'What do you want to say now, Neha? Who is at fault in all those gut-wrenching stories?' Nidhi raised her eyebrows while talking.

'Well. Natasha made the mistake of teaming up with the guy. Priya walked down the street without a boy to protect her and then even went to the balcony after dark at vulnerable spots. Nidhi took off her *dupatta* in a crowded bus and showed off her cleavage. And Alka *Ji*, you wore a saree with a sleeveless blouse, 35 years ago! There you have it. It's your fault. It's always your fault first. Correct yourself first and then point fingers. My father always said that men are sick. Women are the ones who need to be careful. They should dress appropriately and behave subtly; to not get noticed by a creep.' Neha smiled with a sense of satisfaction, proving her point.

'That is just so wrong, Neha,' Priya said.

'I wish that these men were different. It is a severe problem. The worst part is that every woman has experienced it at some stage in her life. But at the same time, I think it can be avoided. Delhi has always been the worst place for women. Despite this, Delhi girls don't learn their lesson. Not just my father, even teachers at my school have taught us throughout our lives that as women, it is our responsibility to make sure that we don't draw unwanted attention. Men will be men, after all. They just can't help it. My father says that girls are like diamonds, and if you throw a diamond on the street, someone will come and grab it. They just can't help it,' Neha tried to justify herself further.

'So, does that mean that all men are the same? If you had a son, you think he would be the same too? Will you not make an extra effort to teach him not to objectify women and to respect them? Is that how all men in your life have been? Your father? Your brother? And also your ex? Was he the same too?' Priya tried to jeopardize Neha's theories.

'My brother was the prince of my house. He got all the freedom and all the perks. He didn't have to look presentable or wasn't *not* allowed to enter the kitchen five days a month. Not that he ever was expected to cook or clean or wash anything. This is my fate. I'm the woman who gets menses, who needs to look pretty and who needs to take care of domestic chores. Men are stronger, though. There's a reason that all sisters tie *rakhi* on their brother's wrists to seek protection every year. Men are made different.' Neha's childhood seemed not atypical from many other girls.

'Shut the fuck up, Neha! Tell me the reason why the same sisters who become wives starve themselves on *karva chauth* to protect their husbands every year? That is the worst part,' Priya raised her voice.

'No, the worst part is that if you wear objectionable clothing in public places or . . . a blood-red lipstick to work or use dirty words in your speech . . . you are just inviting men over. Do you all want to be *those kinds of girls*?'

'Everyone, there is something big trending on social media. It's very recent. I got a notification from my friend,' Natasha said while scrolling down on her phone.

Priya began getting notifications too. 'Yeah. It's everywhere. There's some school-girl named Shikha who has posted it. Something happened to her. Something big. Just a couple of hours ago.'

Natasha seemed quite worked up and enraged. She began to rant. 'Neha. What did you say your husband's name was? Pankaj? Right? He is an asshole. He molested this girl, Shikha Merchant. Shikha was walking down the street outside her school, and your husband slowed down the car and followed her. She got scared and changed paths. He continued to follow like a maniac, and ultimately, on a deserted street, he cornered her and tried to touch her . . . ummm . . . boobs. She resisted, and he kept forcing himself until a couple of people arrived and rescued Shikha and straightaway called the police. Do you know that if I hadn't gotten my hand fractured, I would also be at school, and would be walking down the street outside everyday to get home, all alone? It was just your husband's fault. Not Shikha's. It wasn't my fault that I partnered up with a boy who was eight years older than me when I was just a little girl playing dumb charades at her friend's birthday party. Get woke!'

'It's perplexing. On the one hand, men are-equal-to women. On the other, women have to be more mature, and men are excused because they just can't help it. Neha, you seriously need to think about your perspective. You can't justify demons. I can't always depend on a man to walk with me and protect me from another one.' Priya was intrigued.

'Oh come on, Neha! Go through your phone. You'll see for yourself. It's all over social media like I said. Do it. Do it now. Read her story. This is the exact same thing that happened to my Grandma decades ago. Do you not see the pattern?' Natasha was extremely persistent.

'I still don't have a social media account. Pankaj didn't want me to. . .' Neha couldn't finish.

'Pankaj is a creep. And so are you if you are being an assistant in his power trips and making life hell for others. It's not just a man's world. It never was.' Natasha was anguished.

'Natasha. Please!' Alka stopped her grand-daughter from going any further.

She then continued, 'Neha, does every woman in this world deserve molestation? Do you seriously believe that? Do I deserve to be scarred and scared for life? I am 55 years old goddammit and still have chilling nightmares that something might happen to me tomorrow if I walked down that street! Is it seriously a mistake to wear a sleeveless blouse on a boiling hot summer day? I mean, I am glad this girl Shikha was brave enough to let the world know. If I had done something like that in my days, I would have become notorious for taking action. Nobody would have *married* me. Perhaps, my parents would have had a stroke, and I would have committed suicide or something. But times have changed. You need to change too.'

'That's right. I can't wipe off my sweat in a sweaty public bus because it reveals my *forbidden* body part a bit. But the dire consequence I faced as the man flashed his private part at me is still not at fault?' Nidhi questioned.

'And it definitely wasn't your fault that Pankaj didn't love you and instead punished you for not being *honest*. It was about a past romance for heaven's sake. You don't have to bottle up your feelings,' asserted Priya.

'You haven't answered my question from before yet. What about your ex-boyfriend? Was he like Pankaj too?' Natasha was curious.

'Tarun was the sweetest. I met him right here, on this table. I knew he was attracted to me straightaway. I could just feel it. But he never said it. It was love-at-first-sight for me too. I couldn't control myself. I was attracted to him like a magnet, and he was trying his best to hide his feelings.' Pooja smiled, remembering the priceless moments she had spent with Tarun. 'After a couple of meetings, I was the one who held his hand, and we kissed. I loved him. I still do. But adultery was off the charts for me. Had he been a *brahmin* like me, I would have married him instead of Pankaj. My father was terrified, and he refused an inter-caste marriage. I have been brought up in a very cultured family, and my family would kill me if I ever spoke to Tarun again.'

'There you go, Neha. Tarun was different. Right,' asked Priya.

'Priya, he was different because I never dressed inappropriately in front of him. And like I told you, I took the lead in getting intimate with him, which I feel was a huge mistake. I should have stayed within my boundaries. Pankaj would have been different today. Tarun wouldn't have existed in my life, had I not given him the wrong signals,' said Neha before covering her face with her palms shamefully.

Alka sighed and held Neha sternly with her shoulders and retorted, 'You foolish girl! Can't you see the difference? Tarun was great, and Pankaj was evil. Tarun liked you, but he never acted on it until you made it clear that you liked him too. You didn't give him the wrong signals; you gave him consent. You were both adults. Let me rephrase, Tarun didn't molest you like the boys in our stories. But your husband did it to several women. *Tarun was your boyfriend whom you loved and hence had a consensual physical relationship with him.* That's the difference!'

Priya took over. 'How can you live with yourself, Neha? Drain the swamp. Do your part. It's high time you realize that it's not us and it's not you. Wearing a short skirt or a red lipstick or asking a pervert to fuck off doesn't make us those kinds of girls.'

Neha was torn up. She felt like a square peg in a round hole. She didn't fit in the group because of her mental blocks. Her upbringing had hammered her with substantial prejudice. She got cold sweat and had the epiphany that she had been completely wrong all these years. She wiped off her tears—once and for all. She felt sorry, very sorry, for not being open to the plight of her gender. 'I know now that it's them. It's not my fault or your fault that these men broke us in their ways. I apologize for my attitude, and I promise that I will make sure Pankaj gets what he deserves. I will support Shikha in the argument. I am coming for you, Pankaj.'

Neha opened Facebook on her phone's browser and created a Facebook account for herself sitting there with Natasha and Priya's help. She clicked a selfie with them and put it up as her profile picture. She added all her mobile phone-book contacts to Facebook. It took her 15 minutes. She then reached the setting where the screen asked her if she wanted her profile to be private and public. She chose public. She then posted the first status of her Facebook life. It said, I WOKE UP TODAY AFTER A LIFETIME. I AM WITH YOU @SHIKHAMERCHANT.'

Gossip Queen

The alarm ring on Seema's phone was going haywire, sounding like an off-key musician making the entire house go berserk. Her hand finally reached the alarm *off* button after snoozing it twice over a short span of ten minutes.

She was awake at 6 a.m. but was buried into her phone screen, going through WhatsApp messages from her friends and family—even the forwarded spam so that she knew everything about everything, albeit truth or lies. She took her time to reply to every individual, one by one, before getting out of bed at 7; perhaps to show that she cared. Seema then woke her children up, had them ready for school while watching the Hindi news bulletin on TV.

This was her daily routine. She was ultra-curious to know all that was happening around the world. The issue was that she was more interested in scandalous content rather than real news. She would go through every news update in the regional newspaper, which did not have a credible reputation. She was so addicted that she checked her social media every 5 minutes for an update on top of her secret shenanigans. She would spend hours grasping every interesting detail that later would be potentially spiced up and given a new twist. In her mind, she was a firm believer of 'knowledge is power'. Of course, she never paid attention to factual realities.

Soon then, Seema would take a shower and wear an outfit from her collection of Indian cotton *kurtas* along with matching coloured lycra leggings, *dupatta* and sandals. She would put on a fair amount of make-up with intensely pigmented lipstick and a different set of small earrings every day. She would then fix her hair. All this while listening to the morning news bulletin once again.

Seema would leave strictly at 8:30 am to catch the work cab from under her apartment building. On the way, she would talk to all six commuters in the Tata Innova during the drive. Her conversations would be about the news items she had religiously watched in the morning while others were busy with their chores. She would talk with no acumen but in a somewhat sensational and judgemental manner. Again, she didn't bother how people interpreted it.

'I think that the actor got the award only because he bribed the judges. If you don't believe me, check out my message.'

'I think he is the killer. Why can't the judge see it? He has to be punished asap. If you don't believe me, check out my message.'

'I believe that the pandemic warnings are true and more serious than what the government is disclosing. We should all take extra precautions. Be quick and stock up for the near future. Let's buy bulk groceries before other people finish them off. If you don't believe me, check out my message.'

'I saw this morning that chewing your food for a long time might give your jaws a special kind of oral cancer. If you don't believe me, check out my message.'

'Do you know that *Gandhiji* once said—Speak only if it improves upon the silence? If you don't believe me, check out this post.'

Dr. Madhu, one of Seema's fellow commuters, had advised her on multiple occasions. She condemned her way of life and tried to bring to Seema's attention that her daily information trivia was in fact, attention-seeking behaviour. Regardless, Seema's opinions continued to be a classic projection of negativity, stigmas and apprehension.

Seema worked as a receptionist at a medical centre in North Delhi and being the face of a busy medical practice in a busy part of the city, she was expected to behave professionally. However, amidst the medical centre chaos, she always found time for frequently going through her Facebook, Instagram etc. She didn't care if she knew all these people she was looking at. She just wanted to know everything that was happening in other people's lives. She saw every unrelated post and zoomed-in every photograph by people to register the minute details in her mind and use these for striking conversations with them.

The centre nurse Jane was always seen sitting next to Seema when she had no patients.

One day, Seema asked, 'Hey, Jane. When's the big day?'

'What are you talking about?'

'I saw your sister wearing an engagement ring in your family picture.'

'When? How did you see it?'

'On Facebook. Your daughter's birthday pictures have a family picture.'

'My God! There are at least 20 people in that picture. How did you get to notice the ring?'

'So it is true? When is it?'

'Well! Not until next year.'

'Why so?'

'She wants to study. But keep it to yourself, Seema, please.'

'Yes. Of course. But is her fiancé ok with it?'

'Oh, Seema! Will you let it go? If you must know, he is not. But they are trying to work it out. It's difficult, but she won't change her mind.'

The medical centre was on the ground floor of a commercial building. The five storeys above had different businesses, including cafes, restaurants, clothing brands, boutiques, beauty salons, property dealers and even a gym.

The medical centre had three doctors' chambers and one nurse's chamber who was responsible for the collection of medical samples. Out of these chambers, one belonged to Dr. Alok, who was in his early forties and had a wife and two children. He mostly kept to himself and was generally polite. His patients trusted him well for his medical competence, though he didn't indulge in many private discussions with them.

The second one was Dr. Nicky, a 35-year-old divorced woman who was five months pregnant. She was very efficient. Although she had a good rapport with her patients, she was perceived as *bossy* and at times patronizing in her behaviour towards Seema and Jane. They didn't like her.

The third doctor was a 65 year-old female: Dr. Madhu, who had joined the Centre after retiring from a public hospital. She often shared a cab with Seema. Dr. Madhu lived with a big family, including a husband, two daughters, a son and five grandchildren. She was docile but quite warm and chatty with her patients.

Both Seema and Jane had access to medical records of all the patients. Besides, they were also across personal issues pertaining to doctors and other staff at the medical centre.

'Hey Seema, did you hear Dr. Alok fighting on the phone with his wife yesterday?' Jane joined Seema with a cup of tea straight after reaching the medical centre that morning.

'Again? I think it's the third time this week. I wonder what's going on!' Seema's inquisitive brain lit up.

'Seema, what the hell is wrong with you? I told you I want the three blood results asap. Make it happen today. Call the lab as many times as it takes.' Suddenly Dr. Nicky angrily said and startled Seema.

'She is always so mean to me. Nobody is even here yet. It's so early. I wonder why she is always in a bad mood. Pregnancy hormones, I guess! But wasn't she the same even before she got pregnant?' Seema ranted out as soon as Dr. Nicky went inside her chamber.

'Come on, Seema. Of course, she is frustrated. She has to handle pregnancy and divorce at the same time. She left her husband straight after finding out about her pregnancy. I wonder what could have gone wrong? For all we know, Dr. Nicky might be fighting a big battle,' Jane tried to be diplomatic.

'Uhh . . . I feel it makes more sense to believe that *he left her* after finding out about her pregnancy.' Seema smiled sarcastically.

'Yeah. Either way, he must have done something unforgivable,' said Jane.

'Or, maybe, I'm just speculating that he isn't the father?' Seema's eyes were wide open, with a shock.

'What are you saying, Seema?' Jane was bewildered. Meanwhile, the office phone started ringing, Seema promptly responded, 'Dr. Alok, is everything OK?'

'Alright doctor, I will ask her,' said Seema before hanging up the phone.

'Jane, Dr. Alok is *unwell***.** He can't come in today. He has asked me to cancel his appointments and transfer the urgent patients to Dr. Nicky for today. Oh god!' Seema stared at Jane in disbelief.

'That's fine. I will do that if you don't want to. Don't be so stressed.' Jane offered to help.

'No. I am shocked because maybe he is not sick. Maybe he is making an excuse because of the fight. Maybe he is trying to sort things out at home. If you don't believe me, check out the tone of his voice when you speak to him,' Seema spiralled.

Seema went to Dr. Nicky's chamber. 'Dr. Nicky, the lab will send the results over before lunch. And Dr. Alok is . . .'

'I know. He called me as well. You can transfer his urgent patients over to me today.' Dr. Nicky cut Seema's sentence short and said with a neutral expression on her face. Everyone got on with their schedule after this.

Seema and Jane used to take lunch breaks one after the other so that the reception wasn't left unattended. The one-hour lunch break, which Seema shared with a few other people working in the same building, was her time away from Jane, where she gossiped about her.

'Jane's sister got engaged. If you don't believe me, check out this message. I have sent you her family photo with the ring encircled. Although it might not last, her fiancé disapproves of her life choices. But, you didn't hear it from me. Ok?'

'Another one, divorces are on boom in our centre these days. There's a rumour that Dr. Alok might be in some serious conflict with his wife. But again. . . . Shhhhhh!'

Seema blabbered the sensitive and confidential information to be under the spotlight like a broken record to her friends at lunch that day. Seema's closest friends were Kavita, who worked as a salesgirl at a major cosmetics store and Vinay, who was a book-keeper at the gym in the same building.

'Dr. Alok comes to the gym sometimes. Everybody wants to have a perfect body these days,' said Vinay.

'I know. So, Kavita, tell me about Dr. Nicky's shopping list this week. Was it even more cosmetics this time?' Seema smiled cunningly while asking.

'Pregnant and divorced! She still always wants to buy the most expensive foundations and concealers. She bought three different shades of lipstick last week. God! But who cares?' Kavita answered with excitement.

'Dr. Nicky is a regular at the gym. She never skips Yoga. Sometimes, Dr. Nicky and Dr. Alok attend together,' Vinay hit the nail right on its head. This was exactly what Seema was looking for.

'Wow! Amazing. We should take more care of ourselves too. Dr. Nicky is never nice to me, but she is good friends with Dr. Alok. Extra good!' Seema tried to say something but decided to keep it unspoken.

Meanwhile, Jane left for lunch, and Dr. Nicky left for the gym. There weren't any patients for the next half hour. Seema entered Dr. Madhu's chamber to share a cup of tea.

'Seema, this dark red lipstick is not so good to use every day. Did you see the news about arsenic in lipsticks these days?' Dr. Madhu exclaimed.

'Ma'am, nothing will happen to me.'

'Seema, if you don't believe me, check out my message!' Dr. Madhu exclaimed while mocking Seema.

'Good joke, Ma'am. But arsenic won't harm me as much. I'm not the one who is pregnant.'

'What does that mean?' Dr. Madhu was clueless.

'Ma'am, I don't know how to say this, but since you are the senior-most here, I feel that you should know.'

'Hope it isn't another one of your gossips. Tell me, and I will decide.'

'Ma'am, Dr. Nicky is having an affair with Dr. Alok.'

'What Seema? Where did you get to hear this rumour from?' Dr. Madhu had an agitated voice.

'Everyone believes so. Nobody dares to say anything. But I know for a fact that they are both going out regularly together, on dates.'

'What rubbish!' Seema's fallibility was unbearable for Dr. Madhu.

'Ma'am, he even takes her to yoga classes. If you don't believe me . . . check out the facts. Haven't you noticed that Dr. Nicky is always wearing a lot of makeup these days? Also, even Jane overheard Dr. Alok having a big fight with his wife over the phone day after day.'

'That is an insane predicament, Seema.'

'You don't want to believe me? But then why didn't Dr. Alok come here today after a big fight with his wife yesterday? He is continuing the fight today at home.'

'You are just cooking up stories.'

'Ma'am, I even feel that . . . I don't know . . . Ummmm. It's not very nice. But it could be true.'

'What is it?'

'Dr. Nicky recently got divorced. Just after her pregnancy happened! Could it be Dr. Alok's baby?'

'Seema, that is ridiculous. You better go back to your work instead of making up this nonsense.'

'I'm telling you, ma'am. Even if you don't want to believe it, just keep it to yourself. Anyway, I think your patient is here.' Seema walked out to the front desk to attend the patient, feeling a sense of relief after letting off some steam about Dr. Nicky.

She escorted the patient inside Dr. Madhu's chamber before getting back to the front desk and continued feeling elated at her vicious act.

Dr. Madhu knew Seema was just stupid. But as in the case of every rumour that has ever spread in the history of the world, a seed was planted in the doctor's brain. She had no idea that something which she was calling intangible in her mind today, a figment of Seema's imagination, would leave a mark in her heart of hearts and will lead to a catastrophic twist of events. Also the same way as every other rumour which sounds harmless, to begin with, and gradually spreads like a pandemic.

Days went by, and Seema moved on to finding new rumours to spread. The word that Seema started about Dr.

Nicky was taking shape. From Seema to Kavita and Vinay to people working with them, to people working in other stores to other people eating lunch with these people to even more people who were in touch with them.

After a couple of weeks, Jane finished her shift and called Seema to Dr. Madhu's chamber after Dr. Nicky and Dr. Alok had left for the day.

'Dr. Madhu and Seema, I've just found something massive to share with you both. Dr. Alok is getting a divorce. Can you believe it?' Jane said in a sad voice.

'Okay,' Seema looked at Dr. Madhu and responded in a way that she already knew it was about to happen.

'Aren't you shocked? Well, maybe you'll be shocked when you know the reason behind it.'

'What is the reason?' asked Seema while Dr. Madhu remained quiet and calm.

'You know that my sister, the one who got engaged recently, remember Seema? You already know that she works at the trendy boutique upstairs to gain some experience before she goes on to study fashion next year. Her colleague told her that Dr. Nicky is carrying Dr. Alok's baby. I couldn't believe it when I heard it.'

'Her colleague?' Seema was surprised.

'Yes. Her colleague Sapna heard rumours everywhere about them in our building.'

'Is that the same Sapna who . . .'

'Exactly. Sapna's boyfriend is Dr. Alok's driver. Guess who informed Mrs. Alok about their Yoga classes?'

'Is that why they are having a divorce? Because of what he said to them?' Seema asked with an aghast look.

'Seema, that's exactly right. The driver is the main reason. He disclosed the truth. But why are *you* so upset?'

'Because nothing is proven. It might all be just some big speculation and nothing else,' Seema had palpitations.

'Everyone in the building is talking about it. Everybody knows. That's proof enough. There's no smoke without fire,' Jane added.

'So, it's decided then?' Seema asked with a guilty conscience.

'Yes. Dr. Alok's wife has made up her mind,' Jane nodded.

Seema couldn't believe what she had done. She knew she had to speak the truth, but she didn't know how to go about it. She went back home with a knot of guilt in her throat. She wanted to rectify her mistake. It was appalling how a little gossip went such a long way that was all set to affect the lives of so many people.

Seema lay down at night but couldn't sleep. She kept scrolling through her phone and thinking about all the rumours she started and the ones she spread, despite knowing deep down that they made no sense at all. She either did it as a mode of release of negative emotions for someone or worse, just for amusement.

She couldn't take it anymore and woke up in the morning with a pile of remorse. She just wanted to get rid of the weight of guilt she was carrying on her shoulders. Hence, the first thing she decided to do on reaching work that morning was to confess to Jane.

'Jane, I couldn't sleep last night. I might have made a blunder. Dr. Alok and Dr. Nicky are not having an affair. It was just a rumour.'

'Oh, really?' Jane laughed maniacally.

'Yes! I know for sure because I started it. As a grudge towards Dr. Nicky and I can't tell you how ashamed I am,' Seema began to cry remorsefully.

'Seema, I can't believe it. This isn't the first time you did something like this. Remember that provocative forwarded WhatsApp message you sent three months ago? You sent it to the group chat of the entire building's staff. Then you updated a screenshot of that message on your Facebook timeline. I never said a word to you, but it spread like wildfire and ended up terribly affecting lives,' Jane confronted her.

'What are you talking about?' Seema was confused.

'I would expect you to be riddled. Out of your thousands of meaningless forwarded messages and status updates, one went viral, and it got people like me in trouble. It was about the nurse who made a mistake in updating patient information, causing a medical mishap. Remember she mixed up blood grouping of the parents of the baby and because of that the baby suffered from haemolytic disease of the newborn, ultimately needing exchange transfusion?'

'That was bad. It's about someone's life,' Seema showed concern.

'Oh, Seema! The nurse was blamed initially, but the picture cleared up after a couple of days. The mix up of the records never happened. The mother of the child was hiding the real father of her baby from her family, and hence things took a wrong turn.' Jane covered her face with her palms in disappointment.

'I got to know about it. I didn't believe it. Why would anyone believe it? You are defaming a woman who was already battling her baby's life because of medical negligence,' Seema believed in the sensational story.

'I know it was true because that nurse was my batchmate ten years ago at nursing school and is still a close friend of mine. You escalated the news with such a hype and you, you being a medical centre receptionist—people took you seriously! This fake news spread across the country and beyond. You didn't become famous, but your post surely did. Do you know what impact it made on Indian nurses globally?' Jane was agitated.

'That can't be true,' Seema couldn't believe how vindictivc her actions had been.

Just then Dr. Madhu joined the conversation. 'Seema, you have access to internal information for a reason. It is your job to treat it respectfully. You don't have to sensationalize it. There is no scope for human error in the medical profession. A small strike of medical negligence can put someone's life in danger. However, there are always two sides to a coin. Blindly sharing hot gossip is vicious and an act of irresponsibility. It might have given Seema a feeling of euphoria, but it was unethical.'

'Shame on you,' Jane exclaimed with a stern expression.

'It isn't the first time you've tried to create panic on such a large scale. Remember the pandemic warnings coming from the Southern part of the country last year? The government warnings weren't as alarming as yours were. You went out of the way to spread the fake news. You inflicted immense pain to people of that region. You said they were spreading the pandemic further through import and export, human travel and whatnot. You used every medium available. You talked, you texted, you shared on social media, you forwarded fake pictures—especially that nonsense video which showed infectious people handling rice being exported to us. Remember?' Dr. Madhu scoffed.

'But that was true. I was just trying to warn people of the potential danger.' Seema didn't have a clue what went wrong.

'Don't be naive, Seema. Don't you think that the government is capable of warning citizens of this country? You also sent fake graphic pictures of hospital morgues claiming that the government is hiding real statistics to avoid panic. You said the disease is spreading fast, asking people to stock up on staple food and other necessary items. I'm not saying that you solely were responsible, but you were extremely responsible. You were the real plague!' Dr. Madhu added.

'I thought all that was true, Dr. Madhu.'

'You are out of your mind. Did you have any idea of the integrity of all the content you were spreading? They could have been taken from an irrelevant past instance or even a different spot on earth.'

Dr. Madhu was right. It wasn't difficult for someone to find a filthy place to record on a camera and spread it as the said plaguing location. The real stories of the people suffering weren't shared. Photoshopped forwards took the cake instead. People started having second thoughts about interacting with the so-called *unhygienic* ethnicity.

'People like you made it hell for others. They were held responsible and condemned. The region faced an economic crisis causing depression all around,' Dr. Madhu strengthened her argument.

Seema felt like running away. She had vandalized people's trust, unknowingly. She got a hold of her belongings and left the medical centre in a rush. She reached outside the medical centre and felt short of breath. She began sweating with anxiety, guilt and nausea. She vomited on the kerbside outside the medical centre's building.

'Oh, ho! Seema, is there some good news? Congratulations mommy to be!'

Seema was highly embarrassed. She turned around to see her friends Kavita and Vinay standing behind and mocking her. Seema was extremely distressed now but was quietened by the confrontation by Jane and Dr. Madhu. She collapsed and passed out.

After a couple of minutes, Seema regained consciousness and found Dr. Nicky sitting next to her and Dr. Alok standing next to her with her legs raised, above her head on a chair. Dr. Nicky was checking her pulse. Kavita and Vinay were also standing close by along with a few other people.

Kavita said, 'Is her baby OK Dr. Nicky?'

'Are you pregnant, Seema,' asked Dr. Nicky with a surprise.

'Not a chance, Dr. Nicky,' Seema answered.

'But why was she vomiting?' Kavita asked.

'So you think that since she was vomiting, she is pregnant? How irresponsible to assume! Such gullible assumptions become gossip and then rumours. Right?' Dr. Alok said to Kavita.

'Sorry. It's funny until it's happening to others.' Seema said.

'Are you alright, Seema? Why don't you go home and get some rest?' Dr. Nicky was concerned.

'I'm fine now. And I am sorry about your divorce, Dr. Alok. And also, for spreading dirty rumours about you Dr. Nicky.' Seema was remorseful.

Dr. Nicky and Dr. Alok shared a loud laugh.

'I'm glad you realized your mistake, Seema. We always knew. Dr. Alok and his wife are not getting a divorce. She is, in fact my friend and this entire rumour of their divorce was created to teach you a lesson,' Dr. Nicky said with a smile.

'Yes. The day you talked to Dr. Madhu about it, she talked to all of us—Nicky, my wife and Jane. We made a plan to make you realize the dangers of mishandling even the smallest information. You see, it can have adverse effects causing loss of time, energy and money. Knowledge is power when knowledge is right.'

Footprints

'So, I hope you all have a great summer break! Does anyone have any interesting plans? Any trips planned?' Amal asked her students.

The students in Amal's classroom spontaneously responded—almost shouting and divulging in a chorus, as if the voices were overlapping:

'We're visiting the Maldives.'

'We're going to Kerala.'

'We are going to Nepal.'

'We are getting guests from overseas.'

'We all are visiting Switzerland,' said one of the students.

'That's a beautiful country. I visited Switzerland last year with my sister Nadia.' Amal closed her eyes while saying so; re-capturing the joyous beauty of the land.

'Wow, Ma'am! Did you like it there?' They asked.

'I loved it. It is so clean and so pure. Children, nobody throws away trash on the streets. There is no pollution. The public systems are functional. It is a country where you can drink water straight from the tap and where you never have to cover your face from smog. We can learn a lot from such countries. But of course, it is a different world out there. Not the same history, geography and people. We can't compare apples and oranges.'

'But ma'am, what if we cleaned our country?' One of the girls named Diya asked in wonder.

'Great thought, Diya. I think we can also do our bit to make our country beautiful. Promise me that all of you will never throw any trash anywhere except the bins. That plastic cup goes in the trash. That empty bottle of coke goes in the trash. Remember the saying, Cleanliness is Godliness.'

Back home, Amal's family was looking to buy a car. Amal had a confrontation with her mother, who had picked a car with great mileage. She had gone to the extent of calling her mother stingy. Her mother supported her argument saying that an average-looking car with good mileage is a better buy. It would ultimately save piles of fuel money.

Amal said, 'Mom! Nobody buys a car to save money. A car is not just a utility item. It's a status symbol! We *can* afford it. So why settle for an average-looking car?'

Nadia jumped in, 'Why do we even need a car? It's not like we all can share it to the same spot every morning. The Metro is very convenient for all of us to reach different destinations. Moreover, we live right next to the station.'

'I need it. It's my dream. I've been working hard to save money.'

'You are saving nothing, Sis. You believe in throwing away a piece of clothing after wearing it ten times. You say that it has lived its life and it goes in the trash. You shop your entire wardrobe every three months, including clothes, shoes and accessories. Haven't you heard of reusing and recycling? Imagine the energy consumption required for manufacturing, the new stuff every three months.' Nadia implied that Amal should stop catering to her delusion.

'Yes, Amal. Also, you never even wear a piece of clothing more than once before washing and ironing it. Even a pair of jeans has to be washed and even ironed every time you wear it. It sounds petty, but it all adds up. Environmentally and financially. Even if you are earning well!' The mother added.

'The washing machine will do the work. The *presswala* will iron. It is so easy. We created these facilities so we could live stress-free forever and ever, mom. And Nadia, my looks are an important part of how my students and colleagues perceive me. Besides, I feel it's unsanitary to use a piece of clothing for that long. Besides, what big difference can I make?' Amal didn't consider her lurking around with her green conscience significant enough.

'You hate sharing cabs too! You are freaked out at the thought of a stranger sitting next to you. You don't care at all. Do you?' Nadia wanted Amal to realize the significance of being conservative.

'You are too persuasive! Imagine the monstrous things that could happen to you in a shared cab, Nadia. We don't live in a safe country.'

'Amal, all you want to do is move to a *new country* without even trying to make a difference yourself. You are entitled!' Nadia was defensive.

'Nadia, stop this insinuating conversation. We should leave this country. The pollution, the population, the dangers, the corruption, the patriarchy . . . the list is endless. It makes sense to leave.' Amal took a long sigh.

Nadia felt helpless. She was on a path to save the earth, but her sister's denial and indifference were damaging both the environment and her beliefs. Nadia wanted the world to listen to her, but her sister wasn't even doing the bare minimum. She knew that Amal would change her mindset if she somehow came around to self-realization. Nadia also knew that Amal wasn't the only one who needed to be made aware.

'It is only either you or my student Diya, who think that this country has a future. Diya is 12 years old for heaven's sake, and you are 22. Stop being so cynical. This country has dark days ahead and so is your future if you plan to spend your precious youth like that. Grow up, Nadia and get off my back. This is the end of this conversation. I will buy the car I prefer and not the one that saves some fuel.' Amal stormed out of her apartment.

Amal rushed into her cab, finished her smoothie and her breakfast sandwich on the way, made sure to throw away the plastic-cup with lid and straw along with the sandwich bag into the bin and reached school, just in time. She threw out her temper along with the trash to make herself presentable at work.

She was a middle-school Science teacher. On the one hand, she had her differences with her family, but on the other, Amal was extremely popular amongst her students. She was warm and forthcoming as a teacher.

'Good morning Ms. Amal.'

'Good morning, boys and girls. Sit down, please! Let's begin. I'm reading the first paragraph of the chapter. *Global warming is a gradual increase in the average temperature of the earth's lower atmosphere as a result of the increase in greenhouse gases since the Industrial Revolution. Much of the recent observed and projected global warming is human-induced. It is caused by man-made increases in carbon dioxide and other greenhouse gases through the burning of fossil fuels and deforestation. Adding carbon dioxide, methane and such other gases (that have the potential to absorb heat) to the atmosphere with no other changes will make our planet's surface warmer.'*

'So students, did anyone understand the gist of what I just read from your textbook? It tells you what global warming is, but if you try to look at the big picture here, it gives us a warning. It means that we can prevent global warming from exceeding further by reducing pollution, which is simply sabotaging our health and well-being. For example, reduce air pollution by growing more trees and getting your vehicle's pollution tested on time. Reduce water pollution by not throwing out religious artefacts in the river. Reduce land pollution by always throwing rubbish in the bins and reduce noise pollution by not honking on the roads unnecessarily or using loudspeakers for your events.'

Amal thought that she was just doing her job. It meant nothing more to her, and she wasn't ready to join hands with her environmentalist sister. At last, Amal put a lid on all concerns and negotiations and ended up buying the car of her choice.

Nadia was studying Media and Communication. She wanted to become an actor. But simultaneously, Nadia was also an environmental activist. Unlike Amal, she was going the extra mile to lead an environmentally friendly life. She tried convincing everybody around her to do their bit.

A couple of days later, Nadia came home with a pack of menstrual cups and a reusable sanitary pad each for everyone. She explained how to use them to Amal and their mother. Amal couldn't believe her sister.

'I agree that we should get into the habit of reusable stuff. But no nappies for a baby and menstrual cups seem like a filthy task. You can't keep cleaning it all. You have a life to live.'

'Many people are switching, Sis. See, let me just show you a video.' Nadia tried to clear things up. That was the first time that Amal saw a commercial for a reusable sanitary pad on Nadia's phone and she puked.

Amal was getting ready for school the next morning.

'Feeling better, sis?' Nadia asked.

'Yes, Nadia. I have so much to do at school today. I'm getting all the costumes ready for 'the Good Bad Wood' play next week.'

'That's the one with the gangs of good and bad people trying their luck to win the kingdom in the woods, right? Oh, I love that play!' Nadia exclaimed.

'Yes. Me too! But I need children to help with the posters and decoration. And I've decided that we will also make invitation cards by hand. Call me old-fashioned, but these *e-vites* don't have the same charm,' Amal seemed passionate.

'That's right. But why use so much paper when a text or email can just fulfil the same purpose?' Nadia said.

'Nadia, get a life! There are more important things than just saving the environment. I'm not going to compromise my quality of life for an insignificant drop in the bucket. I'm doing my best already,' Amal was anguished.

'Are you. Sis?'

'Yes! I believe so. The invitation cards are going to be handmade, and they will also have a plastic envelope which says the name of our school, and it will last forever. Period.' Amal again stormed out with her smoothie and sandwich to eat on the way.

Despite the conflict, Amal ended up as a star at school. She handled everything beautifully, and the show was a success. Parents especially appreciated the handmade invitation cards. Amal received the MOST LOVED TEACHER trophy on Teachers' Day that year.

Amal's relationship with Nadia kept getting strained because of the conflicting interests. It was becoming more challenging everyday for both the sisters to reconcile their differences. Amal was finding it impossible to justify herself to Nadia. She wanted to live her life on her terms. And, she didn't reuse anything because she was a germaphobe. She was hysterical about everything. Hence, her motto was to use and throw simply.

'You teach environmental lessons to kids at school, but you never question your contribution towards the destruction of nature, Sis. Why do you waste so many things?' Nadia confronted her when she ordered something from the internet.

'The website had a subscription option, which was cheaper. A pack of 100 disposable plastic spoons, 100 forks and 100 cups for just Rs 250 for a monthly subscription. I use them all the time,' Amal justified it.

'Amal madam, these glass jars can be cleaned and reused for storage. Are you sure you want to spend money on new jars for your pantry? These can be cleaned,' Amal's maid asked her in the middle of her argument with Nadia.

'These are old jars. I don't want to keep mismatched jars in my house. They are all different shapes and sizes.

They are so unaesthetic. Throw them out in the bin. I will buy new ones from Tupperware tomorrow.'

'Really, Amal? Unaesthetic? And also tell me what the point of buying five packs of 200 gm each instead of one big pack of one kg every time from the supermarket is? The plastic packaging multiplies!' Nadia asked with an intensely confronting tone.

'This is so that we eat fresh food every time and portion-control wouldn't be an issue. For example, we consume one pack at a time and are discouraged from opening another one. Look, Nadia, you will never be able to convince me to carry a big bag of empty containers to the supermarket to bring food home. It's too inconvenient. There aren't just goodies and baddies like your favourite play in this world. Think about the grey area too.' Amal tried to rationalize.

A few days later, Nadia came to Amal suggesting a truce. 'Could you put in a word with your school management to let me make a short film with your school students? It's for my college assignment, and I'm thinking of making it an environment-related film. It could be useful for your school's global warming expo coming up in three months.'

'Yes, the Global warming exhibition is on for three days from the 20th of April till the 24th. It's Earth Day on . . .' Amal couldn't finish.

'On the 22nd of April. I know, Sis. It will be good for the school's popularity. We'll circulate it everywhere. I promise that if you sell the idea to your school management, I will leave you alone with your non-environment friendly life. It will change my life. A big career-break!' Nadia had a face begging for a yes.

'Sure, Nadia. I want you to have an amazing career. I will do it.' Amal's liaison convinced her school authorities to let Nadia shoot her film with the students.

Nadia's short film was named FALLOUT! It was ready in a couple of weeks as Nadia worked day and night. The characters in the movie were all played by students. The film was released two weeks before the exhibition to promote it before-hand. By the grace of *netizens*, it had become viral within days. When Amal saw it, she was stunned. It went like this:

The protagonist's name was Amal in the film. The film began with Amal—a high profile fitness trainer in the Netherlands with her family—four children and a husband who were living a healthy life, twenty years in the future, on the exact date April 22—The international EARTH DAY.

Amal had achieved *nirvana* in the Netherlands. After every one of her four pregnancies, Amal aimed to get back into shape and go back to work. All of her children and her husband were incredibly proud of her achievements and followed her guidance when it came to health and fitness.

In the twenty years after her marriage, Amal hadn't visited her home country. She deliberately lost all social contacts barring her family. She even cut all ties with the news, music and even culture. Her mother and sister went to meet her a few times in the Netherlands, but she refused to visit home.

One day, Amal got a call on her mobile from her sister Nadia, 'we need you here to finish off selling our house. We are donating the money to buy oxygen cylinders for orphans. We can't do it without your physical presence.'

'Why don't you move here? When will you realize? Why are you compromising on your health? Why don't you listen?' Amal said.

'We don't want to. Stop pressurizing. Just come here one last time and then you never have to.'

'Alright! If I can't convince you, I'd rather just close the last link I have with that place by selling the house. But Nadia, I haven't visited the country in the last 20 years,' Amal worried.

'I will organize everything to make you comfortable.' Nadia reassured.

Amal left to see her family. Her kids insisted on accompanying her; so, after hours of compelling arguments, she took them along.

Amal was disgusted on arrival as she had expected. The sky was full of smog; the air was stinky, and the rivers seemed like flowing streaks of charcoal circulating to and fro the city; the space was covered with layers of landfill. She was expecting that. But when she saw how the people had gotten accustomed to this life was quite impressive. There were air-conditioned indoors everywhere. There was an indoor stadium as well. There was no need to step out whatsoever.

It looked okay at first. But Amal saw that there was obesity everywhere. Everyone was hooked on their mobile devices, even babies. This obesity was like a pandemic, and she realized the reasons behind it were heart-breaking. Firstly, it was because nobody stepped outdoors because of the plight of the air; secondly, people just couldn't afford to pay for extra oxygen cylinders required for physical activity and lastly, there was no scope of producing fresh and healthy food.

She overheard a lady talking to her toddler: 'Sweetheart! You know we can't play here. It's unsafe. Just find something to watch.'

Another man was talking to his elderly mother, 'Mom, there's no point arguing on the same topic every day. You can't go outside. The oxygen cylinders are bloody expensive to buy. Find a replacement for the *mandir and Satsang (spiritual event)* to pray indoors.'

Amal looked outside the mall, only to find cleaners dressed in personal protective equipment just like medical staff would do while working on a contagion. They wore gowns, gloves, boots, face masks, eyewear and head masks and picked up the waste with tongs. The trash seemed extremely hazardous given there were a few animal dead-bodies, revealing one or more of their body parts.

A scary thought came to Amal's mind—*I brought my kids here! What was their fault? Why do they need to face the music? All this has happened because of people who misused the resources many years ago and had been exploiting nature.*

Just then, Amal saw a cleaner pick something out of the landfill, that revealed something revolting underneath. The bottom layer had a pile of the same invitation card plastic cover, which Amal had distributed to the parents of the entire school for Earth day, 20 years ago. Just like Amal had predicted, it still had the school's name, and it was going to last forever. The card had dropped a bombshell on Amal's conscience. She felt responsible for pollution and liable for the aftermath.

I was one of them too. I committed a crime, and my kids are being punished for it. I did it. I never cared, and I never gave back. I wish I could rectify my mistakes. I took from the environment everything that wasn't mine. ENCROACHMENT!

The film ended with an image of grossly damaged earth with innumerable faces of little children, with tears in their eyes and their hands folded, and then the following text appeared on top of the horrifying image:

Imagine a world where kids wouldn't know what stars look like. Just as we wonder how dinosaurs would have looked, the future generations would wonder about trees and stars and the moon.

'*Twinkle Twinkle little star*
I don't know how shiny you are,
Up above the smog so high,
That I wish I could purify.'

This was followed by:

NOT MANY YEARS FROM TODAY, EARTH IS GOING TO BE THE NEW HELL!

WE ARE YOUR CHILDREN. HELP US BREATHE. CHANGE YOURSELF NOW IF YOU WANT TO CHANGE OUR FUTURE.

Amal felt ambushed after watching her name in the film, but it hit the nail right on its head. After this, there was a link on the screen to a survey called—GUESS THE SIZE OF YOUR CARBON FOOTPRINT**.** She clicked on the link with shaking hands. It went something like this:

Q. How many plastic spoons do you think you have used in your life?

A. >100
B. >1000
C. >10000
D. More

Q. How many printouts do you think you have taken in your life?
A. >100
B. >1000
C. >10000
D. More

Q. How many solo car trips do you think you have taken in your life?
A. >100
B. >1000
C. >10000
D. More

Q. How many pieces of clothing do you think you have dumped in the rubbish bin in your life?
A. >100
B. >1000
C. >10000
D. More

Q. How many times do you think you have turned down recycling a product because of the inconvenience?
A. >100
B. >1000
C. >10000

D. More

Answer these questions honestly, and you will get the answer to the bigger problem which is—

Q. What do you think is the extent of your contribution to Global Warming?
A. Minimal
B. Low
C. High
D. Extremely High

The day of the exhibition arrived, and Amal's school was in the papers. There was ample media coverage, and Nadia was the star of the show. She was giving interviews and making headlines. Amal was nowhere to be seen. Nadia got a little scared. She began to realize that in the middle of all the attention she was getting, she had forgotten to take account of the fact that her sister may have felt cheated. Amal hadn't spoken to Nadia since the release of the film.

Nadia kept convincing herself that she did the right thing by teaching her sister a valuable lesson. But then again, she used her name and pointed the finger at her in the most outright way possible. She helped her sister put things in perspective, but her approach was a bit harsh, rather an unwelcome indictment. Nadia began spiralling—maybe, Amal was just hiding away. Perhaps she was only guilty! Perhaps she was angry with Nadia. Perhaps she was never going to forgive Nadia! Why did she have to use the name? She could have used any name and still sent her message across.

Nadia looked everywhere and finally found out that Amal was last seen walking towards the school lawn. She went outside, looking for her sister with an apologetic mind and a disturbingly restless heart. She was ready to do anything to have her sister back. And just when she teared up with a feeling of self-hatred for bulldozing her sister, she spotted Amal in a corner, sitting down in the grass area by herself.

Amal had folded her knees and hugged them tightly. Nadia joined her, and Amal smiled.

'Sis, I'm extremely. . . .' Nadia couldn't finish.

'Shhhh, Nadia. Just inhale the fresh air that you deserve to breathe in.' Amal looked deeply calm as opposed to Nadia's apprehension.

'Nadia, I have a surprise for you.'

Amal opened her bag and took out a steel lunchbox, full of cut pieces of watermelon. She then took out a cloth pouch and opened it to take out two steel forks—one for Nadia and one for herself.

'You look so pretty in that dress.' Amal pointed to Nadia

'I know, Sis. This was your favourite dress, surprisingly for six months before you threw it away and mom gave it to me.'

'Well, I guess I was just foolish. It turns out that there are goodies and baddies after all in this world.' Amal said.

They both hugged each other while they ate the watermelon out of the box.

Happily Married

Kavita's last convict thought she was the most rational murderer ever. Given she had smashed the head of a random *roadside Romeo* with a rock. He was *catcalling* and stalking her. She confessed to Kavita 2 days ago.

Kavita was my interrogation-in-charge. Now, she wanted to know if I had a good enough reason to kill. Her face was full of anguish. She talked with a prejudiced tone, although she had anticipated nervousness in mine.

I smiled at her with vanity and said, 'Don't worry. I'm ready to talk.' Then, I began telling my tale.

> It all began years ago when Nitin proposed to me after two years of dating. I refused, and it hurt his tiny ego. He couldn't believe *I* was rejecting *him*. It made no sense to him as I was 25 years old but 85 kilos heavy. Nitin, on the other hand, was pretty much an all-ticks-in-the-boxes. What can I say, I didn't feel the kind of connection I should have deemed to be able to marry him. I chose to be happily unmarried until I found the right person. I believe I broke his heart, but I didn't want to say yes out of obligation.
>
> I was sure about my decision. I was young and just like any other girl of my age, paradoxically irrespective of my size, thought that the soulmate of my fairytale was still out there, waiting for me. I hate to admit that I

was naive. The truth is that not a lot of people are attracted to a girl of my size. And if they are, they are almost all of the time either sleazy or worthless in some other way. I didn't find anyone worthy for a long time after that.

But as they say, dreams do come true. Three years later, I found love again. Karan was my boyfriend of almost six months now, and we were going to go on a trip to exotic Bali. I already knew he was going to propose because I had seen a receipt from a jewellery store; that made my heart skip a beat. After losing hope of finding true love, it felt like the magic wand was still working or my genie had just bowed to me to say—*your wish is my command.*

It was happening. The day had come. I was all set to catch my flight to Bali. I kept thinking about my accidental meeting with Karan during my taxi trip to Indira Gandhi International Airport, Delhi.

Karan and I were destined to meet. It was while I was working as a Kindergarten teacher at a high-end pre-school. Most kids at my school belonged to the rich and the famous in the city. It was yet again destiny that helped me get that job via my ex-boyfriend Nitin. He had referred me to the school Principal because he knew the Principal's son. I broke up with Nitin, but I wasn't going to leave that job.

One day at school, one of my students, the 4-year-old Aadya, had a fever. As class teacher, I was obliged to call her parents. After about 40 minutes, I got a note saying—*Mr. Karan Sahni is here to pick up his niece Aadya.*

I asked the other teacher to supervise the children as I took Aadya with me outside, to verify her uncle's identity and then hand her over.

Aadya left my hand and ran into Karan's arms straightaway. He lifted the little girl in his arms and said something to her, in her ear, and she hugged him. I was satisfied with the warmth I saw between them.

'I don't need to verify, but it's protocol,' I said to Karan.

Karan took his driving license out of his pocket and handed it over to me. 'Not a problem, Miss.'

'I already received a message from Aadya's father about you. Aadya seems to be pretty close to you.'

'Yeah, we are besties. Right, my princess?' Karan smiled as he asked Aadya.

Little Aadya said nothing but shyly hugged her uncle. She then looked over to Karan's friend Sunil standing next to him and gave him a high-five.

I said, 'Alright then, I hope you feel better soon, Aadya.'

Karan was continually trying to fight his desire of laying his eyes on me. It was subtle, but I could still sense it. I smiled at him because I was doing the same until they left. I knew we both felt it. How couldn't we? Such things don't go unnoticed that easily!

I couldn't help thinking about Karan for the next four days. He had a charming presence. I wished to see him again, and Aadya was the only medium. I agree that I was a tad bit desperate but only because such romantic encounters were few and far between for *fat chicks* like me. Perhaps the 29th of February is more common than me getting a genuinely romantic vibe from a man. I went in with all of the loose bits of my flabby body and most importantly, my heart.

I decided to give Aadya's parents a call to inquire about her health and hoped to take the conversation further to a point where I would mention that I wanted to visit Aadya at her house. I was going to pick a time late evening so that the entire family was present, including Karan.

I reached school and saw Aadya sitting amongst the rest of the class. 'I am better now, Miss,' Aadya said.

'I'm glad, sweetheart,' I said.

For the rest of the day, I kept thinking of another way to meet Karan. When school was over, I couldn't believe my eyes. A faint figure of a slender man was threading towards me. He approached me with a big smile and said, 'I am here to pick up Aadya.'

It was indeed, Karan. I started fumbling. I had butterflies in my stomach—*Was this happening? Did he plan this? Was he interested in me? Was it appropriate? Was it acceptable? Was it even real? Could he not see how fat I was?*

Karan said, in a louder voice and an even bigger smile, while I was thinking and staring at him, 'Miss, could you call Aadya?'

'Right. I am sorry. I was lost for a minute. I was just looking at your . . . Umm. Never mind. I will get her.' I knew what I was feeling, and I wanted to tell Karan, but I was lost in translation. Suddenly I realized that Karan wasn't alone. Sunil was standing next to him and smiling at me, probably mocking me about how head over heels I was for his friend. I decided not to pay attention and instead ran inside embarrassingly.

Karan took Aadya in his arms after I brought her there and they left with Karan walking backwards carrying his niece. It seemed like a historical scene from a royal scenario where the leading commander Birbal was dispersing backwards from his king Akbar's *durbar* without showing his back to the king. The only difference was that instead of bowing down to prevent looking at the king, Karan never took his eyes off me.

This continued for two more days. Karan and I both knew what was happening.

On the 3rd day, I opened Aadya's bag to look for a change of clothes. I saw a fluorescent green envelope, sealed and addressed to *Miss Shreya*. I asked Aadya about it, but she had no clue.

I opened it, and it contained a folded sheet of white paper that said *Dinner? Tonight?*

I blushed, and I just couldn't stop smiling for the rest of the day.

Karan came to pick up Aadya as usual, but that day he was alone and seemed nervous. He wasn't smiling. He came up to me and started fiddling with his wristwatch. I didn't take my eyes off him and gave him an intriguing smile. I handed over Aadya, who was asleep over to him. He walked out, carrying her in his arms, still looking at me as usual, waiting for an answer. I knew Karan could be the answer to all my insecurities. But I was hesitant because I was Aadya's teacher and he was her uncle. I wanted to respect boundaries.

After a minute, I realized that it might be the end of that as Karan would never come back to pick up Aadya again, given my silence. I could capture the opportunity at my end, as the ball was in my court now. My heart told me to break all barriers and go for it. I looked around for Karan and Aadya and saw them walking in the street right outside the school. Karan had parked the car at the very end of the road, to avoid getting caught in school traffic.

I yelled, 'Aadya left her colouring book behind', just in time to grab Karan's attention. He had entered the driver's seat after putting Aadya into the back seat where she slept peacefully. I opened the front passenger side-door while Karan closed his'. I leaned on to sit down, holding *no* colouring book in my hand.

'Where is that colouring book, Miss Shreya?' asked Karan while staring right into my eyes and hoping for an answer he wanted to hear. I continued to lean and move further, looking at Karan and planting a slender, quick kiss on his cheek.

'The book was just an excuse. Dinner? Tonight?' This time I asked him.

And then there was no restraint or boundary. Karan kissed me while holding my cheeks; his kiss was so tender that it created a sea of emotions running inside me. His desire and his softness moved me. Moreover, he came across a bit nervous, and I found it extremely sweet. And that's where it all started. Do you know how they say that a woman can tell how a man feels about her from the way he kisses her? Well, I for sure could tell that Karan had nothing but love and respect for me. He was so nervous that my heart melted with his innocence.

Six months with Karan were heavenly. We spent a lot more time together. The best part was that all other men who had shown some interest in me before Karan were just trying to scratch the *sex* itch, but Karan never crossed that line. I was touched by the fact that he adored our relationship more than anything else.

Meanwhile, I got to know Sunil quite closely. He seemed like a darling. Sweet as a marshmallow. I was ecstatic to have him as a friend. In those six months, Karan, Sunil and I had become the three Musketeers. *The three Amigos*!

I knew Karan would propose the very same night we reached Bali. I asked him to wait at the cafe, and I began to dress up straightaway. I wore a knee-length mocha coloured sleeveless dress with beige sandals that had platform heels. I put dull golden earrings with dangling-beaded chains that reached halfway through the length of my neck. I left my straight shoulder-length black hair open. I put on a little makeup and added a splash of perfume and picked up my dark brown bag that had-a-golden-chain sling and left. I left for the fantasy of any girl, fat or not, to come true. As expected, Karan asked me to marry him.

Karan proposed to me in the dreamiest way possible. A gazillion rose petals, champagne, doves, music, a giant diamond on the ring—and sitting down on a knee at the exotic Tegenungan waterfall, Ubud, Bali, Indonesia. Wow!

Karan was a champion at getting things right. How could have I said no to him? He was so romantic and so gentle. I said, yes. I just had to marry someone who appreciated and acknowledged my *chutzpah*. Someone who wasn't proposing to me because he should be. Someone who knew that underneath a fat girl, I was a die-hard romantic.

At the age of 28, I got married after being deeply in love with Karan. He was perfect in every sense. I thought I was the luckiest girl ever. At least that's what my mother made me believe. She was jumping with joy. She just wanted me to find a husband.

We had the perfect honeymoon in Italy, and we began the ideal married life after that. Karan proved to be a great husband. His social media was full of *My Shreya* posts. And he wasn't even interested . . . only in sex, like other guys.

In our five months of marriage, we had almost nil quarrels. He was a dedicated family man, and his parents were nothing less than ideal. I couldn't have ended up in a better house. I felt secure and protected. I thought that a family so wise could do no wrong. I was proud of my choice. It was a real marital bliss.

Back to the interrogation, Kavita was patiently listening to me until now. 'That is the sweetest story I've heard. But what went wrong?' Kavita seemed agitated.

'Did you call my mother? She lives in Malaysia,' I interjected immediately, suddenly remembering my mother in a somewhat painful way.

'Yes, we did, and she is on her way. She'll be here in a couple of hours. Please continue,' Kavita insisted.

My marriage with Karan was terrific until it wasn't. I had thought he was the right one, but as it turned out, the marital bliss started bothering me after all. Karan became a busy man after that. He was working late often while I quit my job to feed a classic, rich and mostly a boring marriage. You see, Karan was a workaholic, and I was a typical pathetic housewife whose life went thinking about what *saree* to wear to the next family gathering.

On top of it, we weren't coming close to each other at all . . . I mean, there was no intimacy. There wasn't any time for it—to be honest. Sunil had also almost vanished. I was battling life. However, the catch was that Karan never felt that anything was missing.

On one hand, I was getting desperate to conceive a baby now, and on the other, my husband was never there. Nine out of ten days, Karan left for work before sunrise, and by the time he returned home, I had already slept. This wasn't a *short-term project* kind of a thing. It was a routine. Even on weekends! I consistently sent him texts about missing him and feeling lonely and got just a *kiss emoji* in a reply from him. And after a few months, that *smiley* face became an *angry face emoji* in his responses. I didn't know what to do. I felt like a hostage.

I tried to convey my woes to my mother. I told her that I was considering a divorce. She rejected the idea outright. She asked me to lose weight instead. She said that it wasn't always a man's job to initiate. She said that I had to seduce my husband. It was torturous to hear it every single day from your mother that I wasn't skinny enough for my husband to want to sleep with me. I thought it was just bullshit as my mom was old school. Only, it wasn't bullshit.

I finally decided to make an impromptu visit to Karan's office. As soon as he saw me, he began to rant. He said the worst imaginable crap to me. He called me a worthless person who has no life of her own. He said that I was wasting my time chasing him when my focus should be on losing weight. He said he had thought that I would become less lazy after marriage and work on my body.

He was ruthless. I just couldn't believe that it was indeed Karan talking to me like that. I gave him the benefit of the doubt because my mom would never agree. I told myself that maybe he is acting out because of work pressure. But it just wasn't easy for me to keep playing his happy wife.

'What are you saying, Shreya? A moment ago, you called yourself the luckiest girl ever. Is that it? Karan suddenly got busy? Or is it because he called you fat? Is this why things took a dark turn? Was a boring and sad marriage reason enough?' Kavita was horrified.

'Get to the point NOW!' Kavita banged loudly on the table and clenched her teeth.

'I know that you are trying to intimidate me, Kavita,' I was shaking.

'Ok. I'm sorry. But please tell me why you killed him,' Kavita was losing her patience.

'I was desperate for a chance to come my way, and it did one night. My way out of the mess. Precisely on our wedding anniversary. Karan and I went out for dinner, and while driving back to the house, we met with an accident. Karan died on the spot. That was the moment when my life changed forever. I went back home and mourned for a few days before the family got back to normal somehow. I decided to move to Bali. I had access to Karan's bank account, and I set up a new life for myself there. I started a new company where I sold artefacts. I even met a man who was, unlike Karan, always available, and I loved being with him. He made me feel alive. He took me out of my wife monotony and gave me the kind of love I desired. We partied—we cooked—we went on actual dates and holidays together. We spent a long time just holding each other more than you know.'

'What the hell? Were you dreaming?' Kavita was clueless.

'I was. It was just a dream. Karan was very much alive and was sleeping next to me in the same bed when I woke up that morning. But you know, that dream changed something inside me. It made me feel that I could have a life too. I tried my best to distract myself, but I just couldn't give up on that dream. I kept fantasizing about Karan's death now. I didn't know how to get over such thoughts.'

'So, you did it? Because of the dream or whatever, but simply because you were indeed getting bored being married to Karan. Right?' Kavita's finger was pointing towards me now.

I couldn't take it anymore. The finger that Kavita had pointed at me made me feel like a blood-thirsty vampire. I had to speak up now or be accused as a monster forever. 'Wrong! Have you heard about two sides of a coin, Kavita? Seriously? Why are you accusing me of something without even knowing the real story? Isn't it your job to be patient and make people confess?'

'That's exactly what I'm trying to do. But your story is unbelievably lame. What was your motive?' Kavita's voice was full of frustration.

'Where's my mother? She's never there anyway. Why bother now? Forget it! Yes, I did kill him but . . .'

'But what? Shreya? He loved you. So what if he couldn't pay attention to you? You could have looked for other options. You just wanted to kill him, move to fantasy land and find someone else. You should have just divorced him, Shreya. Are you a child who has to obey her mother? Oh, wait! Divorce wouldn't have left you with enough money. Right?' Kavita's accusations were getting wilder.

I had a million thoughts running across my mind. But I couldn't say anything more to defend myself. It seemed like the end of the war. 'Yes. That's exactly what happened, Kavita,' I said in a condescending tone now.

'You have simply proven that you are a morbid person. Gruesome and brutal!' Kavita put on her jacket and stepped out for a tea break.

Kavita ordered a ginger tea and sat down across from her colleagues—Vikram and Geeta—in the prison cafe. They were a couple. Vikram was a young Superintendent of Police who had recently cracked the civil services exams, and Geeta was Kavita's assistant. They were smiling about something when Kavita interrupted them.

'New lovers on the block. Right? Enjoy it while it lasts, kids!' Kavita exclaimed.

'Come on, Kavita madam. You can't say that. Your husband is such a caring man. I'm sorry if that was out of line,' Geeta added with an embarrassed look.

'It's fine, Geeta. Don't worry about it,' Kavita shook her head with a smile.

Kavita switched on her phone and saw some missed calls and texts from her husband. They were about their son being sick at school, and hence her husband was on his way to pick him up. And the last message from her husband was—*Don't worry, Kavita. I'll take care of him.*

Kavita felt happy. She smiled and replied to her husband—*You are the best. Let's do something asap when our son feels better. Let's plan a holiday.*

She knew they weren't going anywhere on a holiday as she was too busy, but just by saying so, she was expressing what her husband meant to her. She was grateful that he was taking time off for their son so that she didn't have to. By sending the above text, she was acknowledging him, and that was enough for them to stay in love after years of marriage.

She immediately got a reply from him—a *kiss emoji*. She smiled and thought of Karan's text replies to me.

Kavita scrolled on her phone screen to read the texts she had been sending to her husband where she had talked about how busy she was at work and was finding it difficult to take out time for him. He had replied that no matter how much time they spent together, he knew she loved him. She laughed out loud with a feeling of contentment.

'What happened Kavita madam? Care to share?' asked Geeta.

'No! But I can tell you this that you are right about my husband. I guess it all depends on the relationship. One could be 25 like you or 45 like me; the relationship depends on the connection. My husband is great.'

'It takes two to tango, Kavita madam. You are such a wonderful person yourself. How can he not be great? Huh?' said Vikram.

'Well! But it isn't that simple. Vikram, you and Geeta are both in high-intensity jobs. So in future, if Vikram or Geeta become too busy for each other, will that be the end of it or will you hang in there?' Kavita was trying to find some answers and hopefully connect the dots. She knew that I had confessed, but my motive wasn't convincing enough for Kavita.

'We will never give up on each other, just like you and your husband. Every relationship has ups and downs. But if both the parties feel that no matter what the circumstances are; if they are welcomed and needed, if they feel they truly belong, they will stay bonded. We are all mature humans, after all! We understand that at times it could be tough to deliver the exact expectations in a relationship, but even if we do the bare minimum, nobody leaves. Unless, of course, there is a deeper root-cause. That's what I feel,' Vikram put it through in the perfect combination of words which rang a bell for Kavita.

Karan was probably not even doing the bare minimum for Shreya. There has to be a deeper reason. With these thoughts, Kavita abruptly rushed into the interrogation room and demanded to see me again. After some debate and reconciliation, she came to my holding cell. I was in handcuffs this time.

'Look, Shreya. I'm sorry to have ambushed on you before. I think I know the real reason now. I fully sympathize with you, but murder is never an option. You could've sought a divorce and could have gotten the money too. But I guess you are not up-to-date with the laws. However, even now, you could ask for mercy on those grounds. Your sentence might be reduced. Please tell me the whole story. That's all I wanted to say.'

'Kavita, I appreciate your concern. But I can't disclose the truth. The entire world will ridicule me. I'd rather spend my life in prison.' I was crying now.

'What are you saying? Prison is never better. Ain't that right?' Kavita was puzzled.

'Never say never. Prison is better than humiliation,' I was adamant.

'I just have to know this, Shreya. We will go off the record for this. No tape recording. Alright?' Kavita turned off the video recording.

I took a long sigh and wiped off my tears. 'We were in the aircraft, *business class*, from Delhi to Rome for our honeymoon. Karan was holding my hand constantly.'

Karan said, 'I can't believe we are married. You are the best thing that happened to me, Shreya. My parents are so happy. Now all you've got to do is to spend time with them. I want you to compensate for the time that I am unable to spend with them given my work. Just be a good daughter to them, and I will get you everything you can think of.'

'What's that supposed to mean, Karan? It sounds bizarre; I can smell something fishy here,' I demanded an explanation.

'I'm sorry, Shreya. It just means that I know how happy you are to be my wife. I'm as happy to be your husband as well. You do your part, and I will do mine, I will provide you with everything you can dream of. Give and take. Let's just leave it at that.' He kept sounding more materialistic with every passing minute.

I tried to ignore it but I couldn't. I smiled back at him and excused myself to the bathroom. Inside the loo, I took a deep sigh of relief. Relief of being alone for a moment! I felt claustrophobic with Karan's words repeating in my subconscious now—*Just be a good daughter to them, and I will get you everything you can think of. Give and take!*

I then washed my face with the coldest water setting in the aircraft loo and looked at myself in the mirror. I didn't look like myself. I looked glittery and polished like a doll. *I am not that*—And I tried to wash off my matrimony mask. But it seemed to be stuck. It wasn't coming off. I thought I could do this, but I knew now that being married to Karan wasn't exactly going to be a walk-in-the-park.

I broke down, and suddenly I was short of breath. I had a panic attack. I was sure I was going to die. I didn't know a way out of the matrimony cage. The very next moment, a child knocked at my door saying, 'I need to go. Hurry.'

I got a hold of my senses and said to my reflection, 'Shut the fuck up, Shreya. You have got everything in life. Be grateful and behave like a good partner to Karan. Being happily married is the greatest thing in the world. Your mother is so happy. People long for such love and affection. Karan is the best thing to happen to you. Even attractive women don't get what you have now. Stop looking for red flags. He loves you, he proposed to you. Don't screw it up. Be a doll and smile for the camera. The show begins now.'

I gave the benefit of the doubt to Karan. I had made peace with the fact that I was now married. I told myself to not fall out of love with Karan just because he was my husband now and was looking for some dutifulness.

We reached Rome, and I tried my best to give Karan the fantasy of a lifetime. I had made special arrangements. I had bought nightwear I could never imagine myself wearing. I turned myself into a stripper for my loving husband for two nights in a row but felt humiliated every single time after Karan turned down my advances. He said that he didn't have the appetite for it. That he was a simple man who couldn't deal with my expectations! That he would come around if I stopped trying! I called Sunil, and he asked me to give it all a break and enjoy the country instead.

Then, on the third night of our honeymoon, Sunil arrived at our hotel. I just couldn't believe the fact that he had come as a response to my cry for help. I was so grateful to him. I ran up to him and hugged him and cried. The three of us spent a great time in Rome following that. Sunil was a life-saver.

It took me a year. Imagine 12 fucking months, 52 weeks, 365 days to find out that my sweet husband who wouldn't sleep with me, was in fact, *gay*. He was prowling to find a wife that he could manipulate and use.

'I still don't understand the gist of it. I agree he was a monster because he disguised himself as straight. But you think you are an amazing person because you killed him. Right? And it only took you 12 fucking months to find out.

You are posing as an innocent, fat-shamed housewife whose husband never touched her and she never knew why. And when she found out, she killed him. No way! Stop flattering yourself. Like it or not, I will get to the bottom of this, Shreya. I know there's more.' Kavita was inadvertently challenging my story. She just wasn't convinced.

'I didn't kill him because he was gay. I killed him because he wanted me to shut up and continue posing as his wife. And, to make it even more agonizing, my saviour, my messiah, who always came to my rescue and acted like an angel—Sunil, was, in fact, my husband's lover. I know it was reason enough for me.

So after I kept myself awake the night of our first wedding anniversary and waited like a miserable war widow for Karan, he sent a text saying that he can't make it on time. I rushed to his office in a rage. I wanted to tell him that I want a divorce. I wanted to say to him that his anniversary gift was me quitting on him. But, when I reached his office, I saw that it was empty. I knew the gate code, and so, for the first time in my life, I broke my pledge of never to cross the line, and I let myself in. His room was locked, but I could sense he was inside. It was telepathy, perhaps! I kept going in, only to find Karan and Sunil having sex. I froze for a second.'

Karan said, 'I'm sorry to put you through this, Shreya. I didn't have the courage to own it up in front of my parents. So Sunil and I started looking for camouflage. You were the neediest girl we came across. You gave me a happy marriage, and I gave you a fake marriage. Because I know your pain. Your body is . . . let's just say, it isn't positive reinforcement for anyone looking for a partner. So you were lonely, and I thought I could help you out. You know, and vice versa. I knew that whenever you came to know the truth, you would be happy just to have a rich and famous husband to make the world jealous. You try so hard to have sex with me that I feel embarrassed. Don't you have anything better to do? You look like a fat prostitute looking to make some extra cash when you try. Let me tell you something—that sex is not even that important. It isn't even that enjoyable. I mean, of course, you didn't know that because—come on—a girl your size, how would you? You are a virgin. You must be? Right?'

'Karan had added insult to my injury; not only had he patronized me, but he had wholly nullified my existence. He thought that I was so miserable that my only desire was to have a husband's last name replace mine. He felt that even if I were his wife, he didn't have to be my husband. He thought that he could use me as a mask to preserve his identity. He had stomped onto my dignity. He had masked his homosexuality and in turn questioned my sexuality with the same euphemism—I was a *slut* to desire him, and he was a *saint* to resist. And do you know why he thought he could do that? Why did he have the audacity to screw my life? Just because I am fat. *FAT!*'

'He thought he could ruin my life, and I would still make lemonade out of lemons. Then something came to my mind that said that divorce is not punishment enough for this. So the next thing I knew was; I had grabbed the long sharp pair of scissors from Karan's desk and cut open the vein in his neck. Sunil had witnessed and testified against me as he knew I couldn't own up to the fact that I had been such a fool for such a long time that I couldn't realize what was going on. So here I am. I did it. I wasn't some needy fat and weak woman who was obliged to live the life of being someone's trophy wife. I am a murderer. A dangerous cold-blooded murderer.'

'Look, Shreya. You do sound quite bitter. I agree that what Karan and Sunil did to you was deeply unsettling but killing him? You still don't have an alibi to get yourself off the hook. So, I guess it doesn't matter if you keep it a secret or not.'

'I already told you that I don't want to talk on the record,' I said.

'Yeah. I know that you don't want to humiliate yourself. I get that. But I just have to say this. There is no need for you to flatter yourself either. You are still a criminal. You didn't set a good example. There are many other girls in your situation. What happens if your story gets out? I mean, according to what you just said, if a girl wants to escape such a situation, she has no way out unless she kills someone. Think about it,' Kavita tried to explain her concern.

I broke down into tears again. I sat down in a corner on the floor. Kavita left the room in disappointment. She couldn't sink in the fact that a loving girl such as myself could kill her husband over such a trivial reason. She felt strongly about me setting an example. Her brain kept entangling into her thoughts—*Being fat is not a negative thing. Karan took advantage of her and repeatedly made her living days hell. He made her feel weak. But did she have to kill him to prove her point? How could she?*

I said to Kavita, 'the only regret I have today is that I should have killed them *both* with that pair of scissors.'

After that conversation, Kavita sat in her office chair and stared at the wall across her for a while until her phone rang and startled her. Shreya's mother had just arrived from the airport. Kavita rushed to interview her straightaway.

'I'm sorry, Mrs. Singh. Your daughter has confessed to murdering her husband.'

'My daughter is ill. She has bipolar. Doesn't that count?'

'Ma'am, with all due respect, that's a lie. We have her thorough medical history. No mention of bipolar.'

'Well! Maybe I can get a prescription from a doctor.'

'Look, Mrs. Singh. Don't try to manipulate things. Shreya has confessed, and there's nothing you can do about it.'

'In that case, when can I see my daughter?'

'Soon. But do you know why she did it?'

'I have no idea whatsoever. Shreya is a tarnish. She has destroyed my name by doing what she did.'

'Shreya said that she tried to talk to you about getting a divorce, but you discouraged her.'

'Our family has never had a divorce. A girl from our family doesn't just walk out of a marriage because she isn't emotionally satisfied. They hang on to the loose ends and lead their lives.'

'Mrs. Singh, things don't work like that anymore. It's a different era. Just to let you know, off the record, she was in a worse situation than you can imagine. She was not happy. If I were in Shreya's place, I wouldn't hide it from my mother. You are an ignorant mother, and hence your daughter is here today.'

My mother clenched her teeth with blood rushing to her head. She was frantic with what Kavita had said. She took a deep breath and said, 'look, I know. Her husband was gay. I always knew that. So did she.'

'What the fuck?' Kavita felt that the mother-daughter duo was messing with her head. She had furrows on her forehead out of bewilderment and resentment.

Mom spilt some more beans, 'yes, officer. The problem was that she wasn't ready to live with it. Shreya found out that Karan was in love with Sunil—on her honeymoon. She saw them kiss. But I said no divorce, and she listened. Karan and Shreya decided to continue with an open marriage. They were both allowed to cheat in simple terms.'

'Gosh! This is . . . uuughhhhhh! Seriously . . . and then, what happened? Mrs. Sharma?' Kavita's blood was pumping.

'And then my daughter found her long-lost love—Nitin. She fell in love with him *again*. Nitin proposed to her *again*. She wanted to break free now. She was desperate to leave Karan and everything that belonged to him. She just wanted to be with Nitin.' My mother closed her eyes and had a look full of disgust.

'So why didn't she? Why did she kill Karan? And she told me that Karan provoked her by saying that she's a virgin and that's because she's fat. Was that all made up?'

'Not really. I know my daughter. She always said that men only want sex, but ironically she never really had sex with any man.'

'So you're saying that Shreya and Nitin never slept together?'

'They had their ways. But that's not what Karan was talking about. He had got himself hooked on the fact that since Shreya was fat, she didn't deserve love or sex.'

'Yeah. Right. I understand that Nitin must be the ideal man! But why not go back to him in that case?'

'Anyway, Shreya asked Karan for a divorce, and he refused. She kept persuading for months, but Karan wanted her to stay. Karan became the good married guy in the eyes of his parents and on top of that, he began torturing Shreya.'

'How? Why?'

'So that he keeps his parents, their sympathy and their wealth. He humiliated my daughter. So, Shreya simply eloped with Nitin to make it happen.'

'Then, what did Karan do?'

'You have to understand. Karan thought of Shreya as his property. Just because he was the husband, he had all rights. He was paying all her bills, after all. He couldn't see her with anyone despite himself being in love with someone else. He just couldn't let her despise him. He needed her to stay to prove to his parents that he wasn't gay. When he couldn't convince Shreya by any means, he went for her lover.'

'Nitin? What did Karan do to him?'

'He hired a goon and. . . .' Mrs. Singh was in tears.

'Is Nitin dead?'

'No. Alive,' Mrs. Singh reassured her.

'Ok. It's complicated but not impossible. We need to bring Nitin in. He has to testify. That's the only way to prove this. Do you have his full name? Address? Phone number? Anything will do,' Kavita picked up pen and paper.

'I don't think Shreya would want that and I don't want it either.' My mother was sure about it.

'Mrs. Sharma, all this happened because of the parents. Firstly, because Karan's parents whose homophobia made their son go to this extent. And secondly, because of you, who wouldn't support her daughter's divorce to simply get out of a preposterous marriage and look, she ended up killing someone. She murdered Karan because you didn't want a taboo to be a part of your family. You would rather let her kill. Right your wrongs, *now*.'

'Inspector Kavita, Shreya called me and told me everything after killing Karan. She told me what Karan had done to the love of her life. How he had harassed her soulmate and took advantage of the situation! Karan wanted to scare Shreya. So he did something evil. He said he would do it again in a heartbeat if Shreya didn't agree to the arrangement.'

'A beating? Really? Unbelievable!' Everything my mother said sounded pure hogwash to Kavita.

'No. Instead, Karan posted obscene and objectionable pictures of Nitin on the internet,' said my mother.

'And so, Shreya ended up killing Karan. You want me to believe all that,' inferred Kavita with an astounding look.

My mother gave her mobile phone to Kavita, 'Here's the contact number of Shreya's lover. I think it's the right thing to do.'

'Great. Thank you. Finally. Let me call Nitin asap.' Kavita took the phone in her hand and lifted her finger to dial the number from her landline when she saw something and stopped abruptly.

'This isn't Nitin. I think you've made a mistake, Mrs. Singh.'

'I haven't,' said my mother. 'Shreya tried her best to make me happy. She tried to change for me. But she couldn't. I know that now that she just couldn't. But she surely tried to when she gave Karan a chance and got married. She tried everything. She just wanted to build a healthy relationship with Karan.'

'But it doesn't work that way. He couldn't do it. He couldn't sleep with her.'

'Yes. I get that now. But it wasn't impossible for them to have a healthy relationship. And maybe just once, to have a baby. I mean if Shreya could try to do it, so could Karan.'

'You asked your daughter to do that? Just because she is overweight, you thought she couldn't find another husband?' Kavita had goosebumps.

'Not because my daughter is fat,' yelled my mother, before breaking down into tears. She then said, but because Nitin is fiction. It's not only Karan's parents, who are homophobic. My daughter calls herself a bisexual. I insisted . . . a lot, and she tried . . . a lot. But her trial and error concluded that she couldn't find a life partner in a man. Bad choices only make good stories. Shreya made a bad choice. She picked her soulmate; a girl named Nitika. And today, I realized that the only person who made the wrong choice of being in denial and tormenting her daughter was me.'

Concealer

'I think I'm going to try all six of these.' Ruhi said to Tara before walking into the trial room with wedding *lehenga* blouses. Tara was sitting on the couch at the famous wedding attire shop called *Kinari bazaar,* in Delhi's famed shopping hub *Karol Bagh*. Her younger sister Ruhi was to get married in three months.

Tara was a tad bit indifferent to the entire compulsive wedding shopping ritual. She wasn't as much of a help as Ruhi wanted her to be. A large number of young girls walked in and out of the store within a few minutes. Tara watched them marching for their wedding shopping. She was observing her surroundings and eavesdropping on other people's conversations to amuse herself.

'Arre, mummy said that we must get my wedding *lehenga* in a traditional reddish colour.' One of the girls said to her friend walking next to her.

'But you wanted blue,' she replied.

'Yeah but mom is right. Think about my in-laws. These are the norms. Also, blue wedding *sherwani* won't suit my fiancé. He has to wear a matching colour at the wedding. So, we have to get pure red or chestnut. We can't play with traditions!'

Another girl walked in with her mother quarrelling about the budget of her wedding dress. '*Ma*, it's the most important day of my life. A few thousand here and there doesn't matter.'

Her mom replied, 'After that day, it's just going to occupy a suitcase which is going to occupy the precious space on top of an *almirah.*'

Tara was keeping herself entertained with the *plight of soon to be brides*. But she pitied the *pettiness* of such girls who had looked forward to their wedding day since a lifetime. She despised the sentiment of every other girl regarding her wedding day as the *most important day of her life.* In her five years of career as a marketing consultant at a kitchen gadget company, she had learnt that people are easy to influence, especially the newly married ones. She had been targeting married couples to sell the most expensive kitchen gadgets, which were not necessarily the most essential.

Ruhi asked Tara to step into the trial room and help her zip and unzip blouses. Tara rolled her eyes as she knew Ruhi wouldn't stop here. She knew Ruhi was also like those other girls who were keen on getting the *best of the best* for their wedding day. She had already gone through wedding makeup trial sessions at dozens of beauty salons and had rejected some of them even before trying. Another bunch waited to be tested in the coming month. Tara went in. It was pretty spacious, as if it was intentionally constructed to accommodate two people.

'Perhaps all brides torment their families like you in the trial rooms. You aren't the only *bridezilla* it seems.' Tara commented with a disturbing look.

'Suck it up and be happy for me, Tara,' Ruhi's eyes were bigger than her eye sockets could fit with apprehension. Tara began to help her. But Ruhi was extremely angry with her. Apart from Tara's forced involvement, the other reason for Ruhi's anguish was that she had found *the one* guy, but not *the one lehenga* to get married.

A couple of minutes later, they heard an inconsolable baby crying next door. It made Ruhi's nostrils flare up even more with her bridal brain susceptibility. Tara walked towards the adjacent trial room door and knocked.

'Hi, I'm just feeding him. I'll be out soon.' A voice answered.

'Do you need any help? Do you have anyone I can ask for in the shop?' Tara offered.

'No, thank you. I'm fine. I just had to first change his diaper. He is ok now. See, he stopped crying. I'll feed him now,' said the voice. Tara said to herself that why do people bother to have kids if they are incompetent to take care of them. Moreover, bringing a baby to that place was beyond Tara's imagination. *Whatever happened to nannies;* Tara wondered.

Then Tara heard the voice inside singing a lullaby: *Chanda maama door ke . . .*

'Your voice is very familiar. I think I might know you from somewhere,' said Tara while she scratched her head, trying to remember.

'Oh, really? I feel it too. Ummm . . . is that . . . Oh, yes . . . of course. You are Tara.' She answered and laughed with excitement.

'Yess! And you are . . . wait, is that you, Pooja?' Tara was happy to find her school friend Pooja after years. The two were very close friends in the past until Pooja got married at the age of 21, six years ago and then Tara moved to

Mumbai for her job. And then, as it almost always happens, the girls lost touch.

'Wait, I'm almost done.' The door opened after five minutes. Tara couldn't recognize Pooja. She remembered her as the cute, cuddly, ponytailed, timid, a bit chubby, introverted, choir singer Pooja who was not only a simple girl but also a beloved friend. She remembered the naive teenager friend of hers who didn't know how to put eyeliner without smudging and didn't believe in showing off her legs by wearing shorts.

Contrarily, what Tara saw was a new woman holding a baby who seemed to belong to the *yummy mummy* clan. She had not an inch extra body measurement and looked polished from head to toe. She was at par with the Duchess of Cambridge when she walked out of the hospital holding her newborn baby straight after giving birth. She was wearing three inches heels to team up with her well-fitted peach coloured plain corset top with puffed shoulders and a black fitted skirt that barely covered her knees. Her heavily painted-with-cosmetics face and fake long eyelashes looked aptly placed by a professional make-up artist. Her hair was waved to perfection to look natural. Tara found it abrupt and peculiar that she had time to put all that on when the young mother seemed rather stressed handling her baby.

'Hi?' Pooja had been calling Tara's name since Tara was lost in shock with the way Pooja looked.

'Hi, I didn't recognize you. How have you been?'

'I'm fine. Are you still working in *Bombay*?' Pooja sounded cheerful and happy to see her friend. Tara, on the other hand, was a bit withdrawn from the conversation. She found Pooja's appearance a bit unsettling. She was uncomfortable. She had known Pooja since kindergarten as a docile girl, and there she was, six years later, married, holding a baby and looking like a stranger.

'Yes. I've come to Delhi just for a few days.' Tara answered with a distinct unpleasantness. She heard Ruhi calling her. 'Ruhi, my sister, is getting married soon.'

'I remember Ruhi. I can help. May I join?' Pooja asked.

"Yep!' said Tara as they both walked inside Ruhi's trial room.

'Is that Pooja? Wow! Finally, something good is happening. I meant to get in touch with you.' Ruhi was pleasantly surprised. Unlike her sister, Ruhi was up to date with Pooja's current situation. Pooja was a budding make artist, and her social media flourished with her glamorous work. Ruhi followed her consistently and adored her, hoping to track her down and perhaps, finalize her for doing her wedding make-up, of course after a trial.

'I didn't know you had a baby.' Ruhi said.

'Yes. Eight months old. I'm trying to wean him off breast-milk. But it's easier said than done. And as you know that in a public place, it is either a trial room or a godforsaken toilet to do the task. But it is what it is. Plus, I don't have a *dupatta* to cover up.' Pooja was right. People find it revolting if a mother is breastfeeding in public. Almost as if she is seeking the wrong kind of attention. Pooja kept talking, and her persona made no sense to Tara.

'Well! Glad we found you here!' Ruhi exclaimed.

'I had to help a client pick up an outfit. I like them to choose as per their body shape and skin tone. Make-up can only do so much.' Pooja said.

'I was about to ask Tara if she was in touch with you.' Ruhi said. Pooja put her sleeping baby down in his pram and helped Ruhi pick a *lehenga*. She was unbelievably good at it. She knew what she was doing.

Tara felt unwelcome, and hence she decided to sit in the corner of the trial room and gaze at her phone. She went through Pooja's social media profile, and although she hasn't had many lucrative opportunities yet, Tara found it very creative. She had started her career as a make-up artist four months ago. She had catered for weddings, fashion events and even school and college functions. Pooja was highly talented in covering up imperfections of all kinds as depicted in her *before and after* make-up client photos. The brides in her client photos were transformed from flat noses, small eyes, blemished cheeks, wrinkled foreheads and under-eye bags to photoshopped models who looked like angels from heaven, just like you find in a women's magazine. She was also a master of disguise who could turn a living person into a deadly looking zombie by adding bruises and skin peelings and a lot more to people's faces.

'Pooja, how did you pick being a make-up artist?' Tara asked inquisitively.

'You know me. I knew nothing. I had no skills. After I got married, I had to put make-up on all the time. I began to love it. So, I did a short certificate course to learn the technicalities and chimed into every event I got into my hands. Birthday parties, kitty parties, charities . . . you know. I'm trying hard to bag more. I still don't have enough.'

'How about we go for lunch? I'm famished. Ruhi is starving herself voluntarily to get that *perfect* body.' Tara rolled her eyes.

Tara and Pooja decided to eat at a nearby Italian restaurant as Pooja had to return to the shop to help another client, while Ruhi left to meet her fiancé. The baby's pram accompanied the girls and was parked right next to the table. Pooja ordered a walnut and tomato salad with espresso coffee, while Tara went for a medium-sized mozzarella pizza with coke. Pooja refused to eat the pizza on offer.

'What? That's all?' Tara knew Pooja couldn't resist pizza since she was a child and now, she was starving herself too just like Ruhi. But she was breastfeeding. Why was it so important for girls to be thin? Tara felt that something was off with Pooja.

'I have to maintain myself. People won't like me if I don't look good. I have to make a living. And it's a myth that I have to eat a lot if I'm breastfeeding.'

'Pooja, it still throws me seeing you like this. I feel proud that you have an identity, but I also know that this was never your game. You just wanted a happy marriage. Are you ok? And how's your husband? And your in-laws?' Tara asked.

'Of course, I'm happy. I'm finally able to do something with my life. But forget about me. How have you been? You forgot about me. Didn't you?' Pooja dodged the questions and instead sounded a bit upset as Tara asked her about her married life. Tara thought that probably she was having some marital issues and didn't want Tara to pry. Given they weren't as good friends as they were before. So Tara took a step back.

'Do you remember the school farewell day? Your mom's blue saree and your messy make-up?' Tara laughed out loud.

'Yeah! Can't forget. You saved my wardrobe malfunctioning. You were a life-saver. The entire batch of students was soaking wet at the dance floor. Those were the days! I wish I had never rushed into things. Anyway, I don't have enough time. I've got to go.' Pooja informed Tara and began to rush things. She ate her salad within minutes and began to gulp the hot espresso when she burned her palate and tongue a little.

Tara offered her the glass of ice-cold Coke, and while gulping it down her throat, Pooja spilt some of it on her neck. Tara quickly took a napkin from the table and instantly wiped off the Coke from her neck to discover a horrible truth underneath.

There were two bruises on either side of Pooja's neck which were hiding under thick layers of concealer and foundation. Pooja had no idea Tara had exposed them by mistake. Tara then, while staring at Pooja without blinking her eyes saw another tiny bruise on the left corner of her mouth, peeking from underneath a thick layer of make-up, made visible by the grace of hot coffee. She took out a small bottle of cocoa butter moisturiser and more napkins from her handbag and dabbed it on the tissue.

Pooja had no idea what Tara was up to. She was still happily sipping onto the ice-cold glass of Coke. Then, with her shaking fingers, Tara tried to rub off Pooja's make-up slowly, ignoring Pooja's resistance to her. As she continued, she kept feeling antagonized and scared, only to reveal the real horrifying extent of Pooja's facial and neck bruises. The dark circles under her eyes were indicating sore, crying and dried out eyes for a long time after the under-eye concealer had been rubbed off. Her forehead had a small scar on the right side from suturing which was again hidden under layers of foundations. Tara realized what Pooja meant when she talked about *needing* to wear make-up every day after marriage. She felt sorry for her loving friend who had believed that her life was so small that she had to cover up her beatings.

Tara immediately guessed the back-story and wanted to dig deeper.

'Hell! That is grotesque! And brutal!' Tara screamed with horror. She then asked Pooja with immense guilt, 'Did he do all this to you? Your husband?' Pooja simply nodded her head and broke down on the table.

Tara couldn't justify being so guilty towards her friend anymore. Something as basic as a good look gave up all the skeletons in Pooja's matrimonial closet. She didn't just look different and fake; she looked violated.

'Why did you hide all this? I'm so sorry for leaving you alone, Pooja. I was . . . being so fuckin' selfish. I had withdrawn myself from your busy married life. I'm sorry.' Tara broke into tears and hugged Pooja.

Pooja told Tara the unspoken truth of her marriage now. Just like Ruhi, Pooja was in seventh heaven when she was about to say *yes* to getting married, six years ago. She was eager to jump into her marital bliss with a dreamy man her parents had found for her a few days earlier. However, as they say; expect the unexpected, Pooja's married life dropped a bombshell on her.

Her sweet *instant* arranged marriage package deal of a husband who had swept her off her feet with his magnetic persona and charismatic looks turned out to be a beast. When she hesitated on their first night to have sex, he forced himself on her. Something that began as a marital rape on her first night stormed her life with repeated episodes of hair-pulling, punching and even breaking fingers. Pooja became a desolate victim. Unfortunately, a silent one. She never uttered a word or fought back to avoid being stigmatized.

Despite the reprehensible and toxic relationship with her husband, Pooja desperately longed to have a child. She told herself that a baby would mellow down her vicious husband. She believed that some wizard would turn the domestic violence and marital rape into fatherly love. Things moved fast, and soon Pooja became pregnant. The rapist husband didn't want to take no for an answer for sex. So, one day he pushed her away in anger and raped her on the study table. Pooja had a few minor injuries and a miscarriage. Pooja lied about having gone through an accident and her husband repressed from being his usual devilish self after losing the baby.

But bad habits die hard, and violent habits are the worst of bad habits. So, things returned as they were before. Forced sex, punches and kicks for disagreements, mental terror and emotional agony took over Pooja's life again. But she still kept quiet. She was badgered and lonely. She needed a back-up to feel empowered and fight back. A strength! Kith and kin who could uplift her shattered identity. A voice to tell her that such a battle could be won; that it's ok to vilify a molester, even if it was your husband. Without that support, she didn't have the heart and courage to own up her misery to the world. Not even to her parents.

Another couple of years down the path, Pooja found out about her second pregnancy. She didn't want to risk it this time, and neither did her husband. As it turned out, Pooja had some complications with the pregnancy and was advised to complete bed-rest after that. It also served as an escape from her husband's violence.

The one rule of suffering is that it multiplies if you keep mum and refuse to retaliate. But that battle was not an easy one to be fought. Pooja faced abundant verbal abuse, meted out to her by her husband. He cursed her for not being available for him during pregnancy. Not much changed and months passed. The baby was born—a piece of welcome news.

But, Pooja's expectations died a silent death when things got back where they started from after the delivery. As a result, the vulnerable Pooja was losing her motherly desire and instinct. She thought of the baby as a mistake that was now making it even more difficult for her to fight back the father of the child. This turned her life upside down. She failed to enjoy her tender moments with the infant, and it further, like a vicious cycle, gave her a psychological jolt.

Along with the continued torture at home, Pooja's life outside the house almost ended. Phone calls, texting, travelling, food, socializing, laughing out loud, and everything else that gave Pooja happiness was long lost. She became a knot of stress, a bit of a puzzle for everyone around. People started distancing from her. She feigned, and her family didn't see anything wrong with her. Her mental health was obscure to her family.

Tara was infuriated. She began contemplating a solution. Tara hadn't seen any victims of hellish matrimony up close and personal. But she had read that a toxic marriage can be like smoke and mirrors. It seems all happiness, but it is precisely the opposite. The victim can become quite efficient in disguising the bitter reality with sweet smiles and laughter. But the suffering has a threshold for everyone. People either withdraw from such relationships or simply quit living.

'I will never leave you alone again. Let's take him down,' Tara said.

'Trust me; I really want to. That's the plan. But where will I go if I leave now? I don't earn enough yet. But once I do, I can go and take care of my baby and myself. But not until then. His family is highly influential. My parents will be so embarrassed by the stigma of a molested daughter and might not support me.' Pooja thought she didn't have a choice.

'I will help you find a job. You have taken on a path which is the need of the hour. Make-up artists can earn top dollar. We will sort it all out with your parents too. They will have to understand that no stigma or label is so big that their daughter needs to tolerate even a single day of beating and rape to keep it behind the curtains. And you need to know that you have options. There are always other options. But first things first, you and your little child can't go through hell to appease an entitled man. Let's fuck him up. Together!' Tara said.

'You are right, Tara.' Having her friend back on her side gave Pooja a magical strength to face her fears. She had to have a cap in her life when it came to tolerating a rowdy male ego.

She looked at Tara and sighed with confidence before taking out her mobile phone. She then called her husband holding hands with Tara and said, 'The predator will become the prey now. I'm leaving you this very moment. I'm taking my baby too. And I'm going straight to the police. It's not ok, and it hurts.' Pooja finished the conversation with her husband with the famous quote from her favourite TV series: *Money Heist* saying, '*Let the matriarchy begin*!'

Love is Love

Vikram and Anaya were in the middle of another big fight.

'You are a witch, Anaya. You just don't care about me at all.'

'Vikram, all you want to do is have sex. You don't give a damn whether I want it or not! And I am the witch?'It was Anaya's birthday and Vikram had brought her to the tetrapods at Nariman Point, Mumbai seaside for a surprise on her birthday. He tried to kiss her after she blew the candles. Anaya was uncomfortable.

'Oh! Give me a break, Anaya. We have been together for over two months and you still find it outrageous to even kiss me? You are *19 years old* today.'

'I don't want to do it here. I don't like . . . PDA. Why couldn't you have waited till we were alone? Why the rush? And the compulsion? And the obsession?'

'You are being ridiculous, Anaya. Look around you. This is *lover's point*—for heaven's sake. You want me to stay with you to comfort you with hugs. Childish hand-holding is all you need to fulfil all your emotional needs. You love the attention I give you. But sex is off-limits? We are not in the 19th century anymore. We are in 2020, Grandma!' Vikram raised his voice.

'What did you just call me? You are a jerk.' Anaya began to wear her sneakers back on in a hurry.

'Seriously! I feel you're just picking up a fight to avoid getting physical with me. I don't know why though,' Vikram was puzzled.

'You will never know. You have shit for brains,' Anaya said before unclenching her teeth.

'Enough! Clearly, you are either a *homo* or dead inside. Or, maybe you don't have enough room for me. You know what I mean?' Vikram was shooting sharp nails at Anaya now.

'Shut the fuck up! Get lost. Out of my life. Shoo!' Anaya flicked Vikram on his chest.

'Well! Looks like I hit the nail right on its head. Well! Adios!' Vikram waved bye.

'Yeah! And don't you dare lie about who broke up with whom, Vikram. I'm breaking up with you because of your filth.' Anaya said.

'No no no no no . . . I'm breaking up with you because of your insecurity,' Vikram pointed towards Anaya.

'I'm breaking up with you because you are a pervert.' Anaya raised her middle finger.

'Not a chance, sweetheart. I'm breaking up with you because you are a fraud.'

'I'm breaking up with you because I never loved you, Vikram.'

'Go to hell, Anaya.'

Vikram wasn't the only ugly break-up she had had. The truth was that Anaya had been a lesbian in denial for as long as she had known. She would date boys just to prove that she could.

After Vikram walked away, Anaya took a selfie with the tetrapods—four-legged concrete structures, which look like big beautiful rocks. In clear view in the background, she posted the picture with the caption—*Life is incomplete but life is good. #loverspoint #singleagain #scared.*

In another part of the country, girls Deepshikha, Parul and Meenal were having the first drink of their lives with their male friend Gautam at India Gate. Gautam was dating Meenal and he had organized the liquor. They were celebrating Deepshikha's admission in bachelor of Mass Communication in Hyderabad. She was leaving in 2 days.

'Truth or dare, Deepshikha?' Gautam asked.

'Truth.'

'Do you like me? As in really like me? I mean sexually.'

'I absolutely don't. Not even if an asteroid hit the earth and you and I were the only two people left on this planet,' Deepshikha bulldozed Gautam's creepy proceedings.

'I'm still your girlfriend,' Meenal was agitated.

'Oh come on Meenal. We aren't that serious. At least I'm not,' replied Gautam.

The three girls had been friends for as long as they could remember. But Gautam's advances towards Deepshikha had been subtle until that day. Deepshikha was both beauty and brains. She was fashionable and mostly dolled up. And she knew the answers to everything around—somewhat Google-like. On top of her attractive personality and appearance, she was a fitness freak, a meticulous reader and inclined art and music. Particularly old classics were on top of her music playlist. She was a complete package and hence boys admired her and came to her with dating proposals regularly. But, she wasn't interested.

What Gautam was doing was not only bizarre but also obscene for the girls to take in. Deepshikha was ready to give it back to him, 'I'm gay, Gautam. Despite, even if I weren't, you are just not my type.'

'What? You are a lesbian?' He was shocked. 'Can you at least try to . . . Ummm. . .I mean, have you ever tried being with a boy? I can make you . . .'

'Shhhh! Too late now, the infection of homosexuality is incurable,' Deepshikha chuckled.

Gautam insisted, 'But you don't look like a homo, Deepshikha. You are so girly. And, so pretty. I can't believe you are a lesbian. I don't buy it. You can't be gay. Such a waste! It's a shame.'

Proclaimed Deepshikha, 'I am not a stereotype'.

Meenal intervened—'And, Gautam, this is a surprise for you because. . . .'

Parul couldn't resist—'Because he's blind.'

Gautam was confused. 'But, she looks nothing like a lesbian. She has pretty long black hair, not dyed in weird colours. She wears flowery tops and summer dresses, not sweatpants. She has no weird piercings or tattoos and she wears subtle make-up. She is very feminine.'

Meenal was enraged and she growled, 'Gaaauuuutaaaam!!'

'You are so silly, Meenal. How could you and Parul be friends with a lesbian? What if she tempts you? What if she comes on to you? What if she converts you?' Gautam asked in a sturdy tone!

Deepshikha had been frustrated by listening to beliefs such as this one which implied that gays aren't natural. She tried to take the joke to the next level, 'Let's do it, girls.

Let's have a threesome right here and let him watch. The fantasy of a lifetime.'

Gautam's eyes widened.

Parul said, 'Gautam, this was a joke! You are such a narrow-minded prick.'

'You girls are sick. Especially Deepshikha. You need help. Go see a psychiatrist. Meenal and Parul, I'm warning you two, these lesbians are too clingy and too delusional. They will suck you. . . . .'

Parul couldn't resist: 'You know, Gautam, I thought that people were moronic enough to believe that girls can make other girls have their menstrual cycle in sync when they share the same space. But getting their sexual orientation in sync is some high-level voodoo.'

'Homophobia is a bitch. And people like you are the culprits,' said Deepshikha.

'Fuck off, Gautam.' Meenal broke up with him right then and there.

Deepshikha reached Hyderabad two days later. She had made all arrangements beforehand. She had booked a room in the college hostel that she was sharing with another girl. She didn't know what Hyderabad had in store for her.

The first time Deepshikha laid her eyes on Anaya was when she arrived in her double occupancy room. Deepshikha felt like a breeze of chilly wind on a freezing winter morning had awakened her from inside out. Her world had frozen. She couldn't take her eyes off Anaya. Anaya's timid and slender body looked dreamy in the black tank top and army print cargo pants. Her bare feet looked out of the world beautiful in the nude coloured nail-paint that Anaya was wearing. Her facial features were sharp and well defined. Her hair was shoulder length and brown tinted. Deepshikha couldn't help herself. She was staring at Anaya with a yearning hope like a poodle would stare at its owner returning from a long vacation.

Anaya was on the phone. 'No, baby! I'm fine. Some girl. I don't know yet. Yes, I'll talk to you later. Love ya. Bye!'

'Hi, I'm Deepshikha.' she smiled and extended her hand for shaking hands.

'Hi. I'm Anaya! Sorry, that was my boyfriend. He's a little too much. It's a new relationship. Too mushy! I hope you don't mind.'

'Oh no. I love mush,' Deepshikha replied with a friendly smile, speaking without thinking, both shook with Anaya's boyfriend and yet fulfilled with the buff of crushing on someone. The girls shook hands and Deepshikha jumped out of her skin. She was taken aback with what a stranger had done to her in a matter of minutes. She knew Anaya was the answer to her romantic quest. She finally knew what Meenal and Parul had been talking about whenever they had a crush on a guy. All because a girl shook hands with her. Not just any girl, but the most attractive girl Deepshikha had ever seen.

But then there was Anaya's boyfriend. And there was the stigma that a homosexual could *convert* a heterosexual person. So, Deepshikha decided to bottle up her feelings. But she couldn't help the butterflies in her stomach which were going *cuckoo* with exhilaration. She hadn't felt anything like this ever before.

A few days down the line, Deepshikha and Anaya became good friends. Deepshikha was enjoying the closeness with the girl of her dreams. She didn't want to *jinx it* by owning up the truth as there was no scope. She found her solace in friendship.

Anaya thought of Deepshikha as her best friend and adored her. She always kept her place in class and the hostel mess. She would never leave the room in the mornings without Deepshikha's approval of her look. She would post captions such as #bestie, #bff, #friendshipgoals against the photos of the duo on Instagram and Snapchat. Deepshikha kept staring at the selfie that Anaya had posted everywhere with Charminar in the background and Deepshikha and Anaya in the frame, smiling and looking at each other. She had captioned it: *my ever lost but newly found soulmate. #charminar #stillscared.*

Anaya would even give hugs to Deepshikha for simply no reason and without any inhibitions. She would go through Deepshikha's closet and pick clothes for her to wear and pass comments like—*You're killing me with your look* and even *I wish I could eat you up Deepshikha!* She was flirting with her. Deepshikha was having the time of her life. She didn't want the mind-boggling magic to stop. She had longed her entire life to feel like this.

Friendship or something more, Deepshikha was feeling extremely elated and she was enjoying the affection. She hadn't experienced anything like this before. Even if Cupid was only answering her call partially, she was still ok with whatever share of happiness she was getting in her life.

She was clueless about why a straight girl was trying to come so close to her. Moreover, her worst fear was of developing serious feelings for and then getting *friend-zoned* by Anaya. Regardless, Deepshikha didn't want it all to stop. So she decided not to behave alarmed.

One day, Anaya and Deepshikha were having a classic *Delhi versus Mumbai*. This was a common way for both of them to strangely connect and bond.

'What's so great about the Gateway of India anyway? Have you been to the India Gate? That's a real beauty.' Deepshikha scoffed.

'The Taj Mahal and Golden temple are beautiful. India Gate is just like any other memorial. I respect the *Amar Jawan Jyoti* from my heart but, speaking as the devil's advocate, the building is lame,' Anaya tried to make a point.

'You *Mumbaikars* are lame. India Gate is my favourite monument. I'm a *sensitive* person. I feel something when I'm there. I have childhood memories. It's incomparable and this argument is irreconcilable. Change the topic.' Deepshikha sounded serious and hence, Anaya switched topics.

'Oh, I hate how Delhi girls are always so pretty. I mean, who wears a cocktail dress to the mall?' Anaya said.

'And girls from Mumbai are so naive. They think that since they could walk back home at 1 am in their city, they could do that everywhere. Do your homework. You need to know the rules.'

'Delhi people are made of butter chicken and scotch.'

'Mumbai people are made of *drugs* and *smoke*. Like that boyfriend of yours.'

Anaya's smile turned upside down. 'He's coming this Friday.'

'So why the frown? I'm sure it isn't a moment to be sad.'

'You don't understand, Deepshikha. He's not coming here to bring a teddy bear and some chocolates for me. He has his reasons. Man! Another break-up on the cards,' Anaya seemed perturbed as she was biting her nails. Deepshikha knew what Anaya was trying to say and yet trying to hide.

'Really? I thought you were serious about him. But it seems like you don't want to. . . . Ummm. . . .'

'Exactly! I don't need him to come over. All he wants is to have sex,' Anaya said.

'And you don't?' Deepshikha asked Anaya.

'Not yet. I want feelings first. You can say that Mumbai girls are old school now.'

'Enough with your Delhi versus Mumbai girls. Let's leave. The movie begins in 30 minutes . . .' Avni said who lived in the hostel room next door. But she was always found in Deepshikha and Anaya's room.

At lunch, after the movie was over, Avni began pushing Anaya.

'So, what exactly is the problem between boyfriends and you? Why don't you ever wanna do it with anyone? And your current boyfriend is *drool-worthy*, Anaya. You'd be a fool not to . . . give him your flower. Like we are in the 70s.'

'Don't even mention that jerk. I'm going to break up with him. Too much mush.'

'So, while you've decided to break up, why not do it once and get over with it? Your first time will be with someone so dashing.'

'I told you. I don't want to have sex before being sure about the guy. I don't care how good-looking he is.'

'It's not a big deal, Anaya. Sex is no longer a taboo. Grow up!' Avni thought she just tried to help her friend when in reality, she was putting a lot of pressure on Anaya. Peer pressure could be catastrophic.

'I don't care. I will have it when I want to,' Anaya put her foot down.

'Oh come on, Anaya. Don't behave like a grandma. Sex is not scotch. It doesn't taste better with time.' Avni kept persisting.

'Why are you tormenting her, Avni. Sex isn't everything,' Deepshikha added.

'Goodness! Deepshikha, have you had sex? Ever?' Avni asked.

'Yes. I have. Now shut up and eat,' Deepshikha couldn't tolerate Avni's tactics.

That night before bed, Deepshikha and Anaya were sitting in their room when Avni entered with a bottle of wine and three glasses. 'I just feel like it.'

The girls drank and finished the entire bottle. Anaya was the drunkest.

She started talking in euphoria, 'How good is this sex, girls? And orgasm? What's the deal with that?'

'Oh, I hope you have had an orgasm if not sex, Anaya. Tell me you have?' Avni intrigued.

'Shut up, Avni. Anaya is a person. Why are you so obsessed with sex?' Deepshikha was worked up.

'First of all, I don't think you've ever had it, Deepshikha. And secondly, I'm Anaya's friend. I want her to experience it. It's important to test your sexual compatibility with a guy before a life-long commitment,' Avni responded.

'With a guy?' Anaya laughed out loud.

'So? You mean you would want to do it with a girl?' Avni asked Anaya while Deepshikha couldn't believe what Anaya had just said.

'Who knows? I've never dared to give it a go. But it sounds fun,' Anaya had no control over her words. They came out like a meteor shower. Deepshikha's eyes were widened. Her heartbeat had increased and her palms became sweaty. Her mouth became dry and she tried her best to control the happy smile on her face. Anaya was talking about being with a girl and Deepshikha was in seventh heaven.

'But it sounds yuck. Girls were meant to fuck boys and not girls. I truly believe it. Anatomy proves it,' Avni said angrily.

'Ok. I think it's best to stop right here. Anaya, go to sleep.' Deepshikha said authoritatively and Avni left the room straightaway.

Deepshikha tried her best to fight her conceptions for a couple of hours and then, Anaya woke up and came to Deepshikha's bedside. She hugged Deepshikha who pretended to be asleep. Deepshikha couldn't disclose her feelings so she put up a fight with herself. She had the uncontrollable urge to kiss Anaya right then and there not only because she had a major crush on her, but more importantly to make use of the only opportunity of ever doing so. She was sure about it. But at the same time, she didn't want to lose Anaya as a friend. After all, Avni had pigeonholed her reality and said the derogatory YUCK for lesbian relationships. She was in a dilemma. She kept swinging between—'*go for it'* and '*have you lost your mind'*?

Then suddenly, while the intensity of emotions mixed with the chaos of feelings going inside Deepshikha's mind made her bring her face closer to Anaya, still not close enough, Anaya took the lead. Anaya planted a warm kiss on Deepshikha's lips. Deepshikha could hear violins. The violins she had been holding on to her entire life after she had seen a boy kiss a girl in a movie. The violins whose existence Deepshikha had been wondering about. Her heart was racing and she was jumping with joy deep inside. She was humming her favourite Bollywood song in her mind now—

lag ja gale ke
Phir ye
Haseen raat ho na ho
Shayad phir is janam mein
Mulaqat ho na ho. . . .

And just then, without uttering a single word, Anaya went to her bed and went back to sleep. Within moments she was peaceful. Deepshikha sat by her side and watched her, all night with a smile.

The next morning, Deepshikha woke up sitting on the floor next to Anaya's bed. It was the brightest morning of her life. She put on her running clothes and shoes and went out with a smile from ear to ear.

That morning run was the happiest run for Deepshikha ever. She was talking to the flowers on her way, she was singing with the birds—she was jumping with the children running around. She was full of the joys of spring. She listened to her favourite songs and even danced a while without feeling constrained or even embarrassed in the park with her earphones on. She played *Antakshari* with a gang of housewives who had come for their morning walk and sang all happy songs:

I'm going to paint my nails
And put my make-up on
It's Friday night and I won't be long

She even had a morning dance party with them in the park. She then bought two cups of Caffe mocha from Starbucks along with two chicken sandwiches and 2 strawberry cheesecakes and was all set to have her first *breakfast in bed* with the girl she now knew she loved and not just had a crush on.

On reaching the hostel, Deepshikha saw Anaya standing, leaning onto the balcony door. Anaya had just come out of the shower and was wearing beige coloured cargo pants with a black coloured tee that had the word *Girly* printed on it in white. Water was still dripping onto Anaya's shoulders from her semi-dried hair and Deepshikha thought to herself—*oh you beautiful girl, why don't you ever dry your hair enough?* She just wanted to kiss Anaya again and relive the cherished moment from last night. And just then, Anaya looked at her and their eyes met. Deepshikha knew Anaya felt the same connection.

Deepshikha said to Anaya, 'Anaya, I don't know what to call it but this feels right. And true. And amazing. You know, the first time I saw you in this room wearing that army printed cargo pants, I felt havoc, mayhem inside my body. I was confused and hence I kept it to myself. I discouraged myself to feel that way about you. But now, I feel that I can touch you without feeling that knot of stress in my throat. That I can be with you and not give a damn about the world. That I can just let myself be and . . .'

Before Deepshikha could progress any further, Avni walked in and sat down at the chair next to the study desk.

'Hey Deepshikha, I was just telling Anaya that she should say yes to Purab. Who sends flowers to girls these days? I'm telling you that Purab genuinely likes Anaya. What do you think?' Avni looked at Deepshikha waiting for her to answer as Deepshikha was speechless and even a bit remorseful.

'The more important thing is what Anaya thinks,' Deepshikha swallowed her emotions and said with a low voice as she put down the breakfast and coffee on the study table.

'Oh please Deepshikha, just look at the goddamn orchids. They mean true feelings.' Avni pointed at the big bunch of purple orchids above that were tied with a beautiful pink satin ribbon in a perfect bow kept next to the breakfast on the study table. Deepshikha hadn't noticed them before.

Deepshikha was shocked to the core. She tried to remember as to why she did not see it coming. Then she remembered a blurred memory. A few days ago, Anaya told Deepshikha and Avni that Purab from college had asked her out. On knowing about her having a boyfriend at the time, Purab had politely backed off. But Deepshikha remembered Avni reading out Purab's text aloud while she had chosen not to pay attention to it and instead simply continued checking her gorgeous roommate out.

The text had said—*I wish I'm the first one you call when you break up with him.*

Recalling the bitter memory, Deepshikha asked Anaya, 'Did you call Purab after your break-up?'

Anaya replied hesitatingly, 'I. . . . I did. Just, this morning. You weren't even here. Avni asked me to.'

'Really? Avni asked you to call and you did? I have nothing to say to you,' Deepshikha stormed out of the room. She felt claustrophobic. She went to the balcony to get some fresh air, and there she silently cried. She knew why Anaya had done it. She knew that Anaya didn't want to be a lesbian. She knew that she was putting her friendship at stake with the kiss last night. She knew she had lost the chance of being Anaya's lover and even being her friend. On top of it, she was confused and utterly humiliated. It was pandemonium!

Days passed and Anaya behaved as if nothing had happened. She began dating Purab and surprisingly, Purab was patient enough to wait to get intimate. But as expected, Anaya was under peer pressure to expedite things. Especially and exclusively with Avni.

'I'm telling you, Anaya. You must do it asap. If you don't fix it right now, who knows you might end up doing it with a girl as you said? And you might even enjoy it. That's exactly how 90 per cent of straight people turn gay. By experimenting. It's not natural and we aren't in prison that we must be tempted to do it. Gays are sad and lonely people who can't get attention from the opposite gender due to their incompetencies. Unfortunately, these homos are ubiquitous. Don't fall for that shit,' Avni's hand was on Anaya's shoulder with compassion. Deepshikha's eyes were on Avni's hand and she was just holding on to her urge to give it back to Avni.

'What are you talking about, Avni? I'm with Purab. Everyone knows that,' Anaya reassured Avni and gave Deepshikha a warning look.

'You need to take it to the next level with Purab, babe! He's not going to wait forever. Just do it. It's not that hard. Things will streamline after you've done it once. Purab is a sweet guy. He's perfect for this. Promise me you'll go for it,' Avni compelled Anaya.

'Alright. I think I should just . . . you know, forget about electricity and chemistry. I promise you that I'll do it. Tomorrow.' Avni and Anaya hugged and celebrated as if Anaya had scored a century on-field and Anaya was her partner batsman. Deepshikha's nose was flaring and her teeth were clenched.

Deepshikha had become numb to the situation. She had kept the memory of that night in a hidden cave in her brain so that it doesn't bother her anymore. She slept with her face turned away from Anaya's bed. But she kept justifying Anaya by telling herself that maybe, just maybe, Anaya was extremely hungover and didn't know what she was doing or whom she was kissing. Or maybe, Anaya was just scared to come out to the world. Either way, Anaya had hurt Deepshikha.

Despite all that had happened and all that was happening, Deepshikha couldn't get Anaya out of her heart. That night, after Anaya went to sleep, Deepshikha knocked at Avni's door. Avni woke up from sleep and opened the door rubbing her eyes. Deepshikha groped Avni and pushed and shoved her against the wall with her forearm.

'What the hell is this Deepshikha?' Avni was shocked.

'You rotten witch! Gays are as natural as your sick homophobic psychology. Don't you dare feed that crap to Anaya. She has the right to decide. Let her take her time. If and when she wants to do it, she will, with whoever she wants.'

'Why do you care so much? Huh? I know that you and Anaya made out the other night. But she was drunk and out of her mind. But, you're making me doubt that even you are . . .'

'Yes! I am a lesbian,' Deepshikha owned up.

'Yuck! Really!' Avni was bemused and began to push her away.

Deepshikha was enraged. She felt like someone with a contagious disease. She saw disgust and repression on Avni's face for her. She wanted to punch her as her first instinct but, on the other hand, she knew exactly what to do.

Deepshikha moved her face close to Anvi's and whispered in her ear, 'If you ever pressurized Anaya to have sex again, I will do to you what you're most scared of. I will not hurt you. But I would kiss you. And trust me that would feel like the best kiss you've ever had. So be mindful!' Deepshikha went back to her room and slept peacefully after that.

The next two days were weird for Deepshikha. Although Anaya behaved like she remembered nothing, ironically, all the eagerness about being besties and the uncalled for flirting from Anaya stopped abruptly. Deepshikha began to feel that Anaya had withdrawn herself from the relationship. Then, Deepshikha realized that it wasn't only

Anaya who was boycotting her. The entire batch of students wanted nothing to do with Deepshikha.

Deepshikha was getting tagged in LGBTQ hashtags and posts from everyone she was connected with on social media. She saw how brutal her peers were. And then she came across Avni's post where she had clearly said that her friend Anaya has been a victim of sexual assault from her roommate who tried to enforce a kiss on her. She saw *#metoo* and she lost her mind.

She straightaway confronted Avni and Anaya and Anaya claimed for the incident to have happened as posted by Avni.

'Why are you doing this, Anaya? Being scared to own up your identity to the world is one thing. But why ruin my life?'

'Avni saw me crying 2 days ago. I didn't know what else to do. I had to tell her that you kissed me. I never meant for her to spread the news to everyone.'

'Why were you crying?'

'Because of our little incident after I drank illegitimately and then in the middle of the night . . .'

'Yes. We kissed. It was beautiful,' Deepshikha took Anaya's hands into hers.

'I'm not a lesbian, Deepshikha,' Anaya withdrew herself.

'Yes, she's not a lesbian like you,' Avni added.

'You weren't crying because you felt molested. You were crying because you felt alive after coming so close to me and then you realized that you would be labelled a lesbian. That scared the shit out of you and that's why you were crying. You've made me a sexual molester. I'm devastated. I have nothing to say to you, Anaya.'

'Don't you dare Deepshikha. I'm here to protect her. You can't force her into your plague,' Avni was pretending to play Anaya's saviour.

'I never considered you a friend, Avni. To hell with you,' Deepshikha said.

'Deepshikha, I'm sorry. I don't want you to think. . . .'

Deepshikha didn't let Anaya finish. 'Shut the fuck up, Anaya. FYI, I fell for that kiss and I fell in love with you. I was so stupid. I'm not ashamed to say that I like women. But I'm ashamed to own up that I love you, Anaya. You are a lying bitch who screwed my life. You're not worth it.'

Deepshikha packed her luggage and headed straight back to Delhi. She quit her Hyderabad college mid-year and began to look for a new course in Delhi. She was perplexed and completely out of the desire to achieve anything after Anaya broke her heart. Her life had gone haywire. She began working as a salesperson in a luxury boutique in Delhi for the time being.

Although Anaya was out of sight for Deepshikha, she wasn't out of her mind. She kept fiddling with Anaya's Instagram and going through every detail. She just couldn't digest the fact that Anaya was still staying happy and telling the world about it repeatedly.

Meanwhile, Anaya travelled to many cities. Her Instagram wall was full of pictures with someone, just as it always was. It was as if Anaya was scared to post any solo photos. Her selfies included Konark temple, Mysore Palace, Victoria Memorial, Golden Temple and Hawa Mahal. The only thing common except her love for monuments in all her posts was *#stillscared.* The only sensible explanation that Deepshikha could make out of it was that Anaya was still scared about breaking up with every new boyfriend for the same reason.

Since Purab stopped appearing in any of the photos after Victoria memorial, Deepshikha started wondering about the reason Anaya had posted all solo photos after that. Her Instagram post hashtags expressed her state of mind clearly. She was alone. She had given up on love and was still scared.

The next day, Anaya posted a solo picture with the Taj Mahal. This time, her caption said: A reason to live #single #again #notscaredanymore #longlostsoulmate #7pm #delhi #atyourfavouritespot #illbewaiting #loveislove. Deepshikha saw the time at 5 p.m. and did what she had to do.

At India Gate, at 7 p.m., Deepshikha saw Anaya wearing *the* army print cargo pants and *the* black tank top. She was standing next to the *Amar Jawan Jyoti.* Deepshikha ran up to her. Anaya saw Deepshikha and straightaway she took her hands and planted a tender kiss on her lips. She then said, 'look into the camera'.

Deepshikha looked up at the selfie stick and Anaya took a selfie with her with India Gate in the background. She immediately posted the photo onto her Instagram with the caption: Found my long lost soulmate #notsingleanymore #notscaredanymore #loveislove #loveisher.

Anaya further said, 'I tried hard. But I couldn't fake love anymore. After you left and I forced myself to sleep with Purab, I realized how ugly things could get. I abruptly left him and found . . . as they say . . . my true calling. But I was scared to come out. So, I thought I'd rather fly solo. But I couldn't shake the emotions I felt for you. I just had to come. I want to be with you. Labels mean nothing to me anymore. You are my true love.'

Deepshikha's eyes were wet; her broken heart was restored. She pulled Anaya's face close to hers and the girls kissed each other with love, as sacred as the Ganges.

The End of Carpe Diem

An epistle to my children

Dear Arjun and Meesha,

Ten years hence when you will be 15 and 13 respectively, this letter will serve as a memoir of a strange and unprecedented time in our lives. This was 2020 when Coronavirus hit and locked down the entire world! Aristotle had once said, 'It is during our darkest times that we must focus to see the light.' Little did he know that it is easier said than done. But kids, we gave it our best shot when it began, and we are still giving it our best shot every day. We are merely hoping that there must be light at the end of this dark, darker than your mother's coffee, tunnel!

Call it Claudius of *Hamlet* or Iago of *Othello* or *the* Jafar *of Aladdin*, or the demon *Mephistopheles* or the supervillain *Joker*; Coronavirus makes them all look trivial. This virus seems to be by far the worst of villains, one that we can neither see nor touch! An enigma! One that is leaving an indelible mark on every living soul! The disease itself as also its ramifications is bizarre—the social distancing, the quarantine, the supermarket marathon, the cornucopia of supplies in the fridge, the endless cooking, the WFH (Work from Home) and the HBL (Home-based Learning). Oh, the ache of HBL was so underestimated!

In light of recent events, I experienced tremendous chaos and commotion in my own house. As a mother of two,

I'm proudly calling it by far the most strugglesome and utterly tortuous parenting battle. Undoubtedly, being homebound with my children is the reason for my frustration. With school now being delivered via videos and apps, I ought to be a fully equipped and functional part of the learning. From good old-school stationery supplies to your personal assistant 'Google', nothing works! Not unless I make it work for you both. Which means that I don't have a life of *my own*!

Despite all the hassle and battle with homeschooling, I am, rarely, able to somewhat accomplish daily tasks. I then sit down with my compromised cup of *non-gourmet*, made out-of-a-pod espresso to get a breather. But, once a mother, always a mother! Within milliseconds, you come hovering. While one of you jumps into my lap, the other one curbs jealousy by ending on my shoulders. Just then, while I manage to put my cup aside and gain some momentum to deal with the imbalance, you ask me the one question, '*can we please get a pet as soon as the lockdown is lifted? Pretty please!! Remember your promise, Mamma!*'

I promised you for sure. But it was one of my fake parenting promises to get you off my back. In my defence, I love pets. I love my sister's little pug a lot. But I can't have myself feeding and cleaning up after another little living soul in my family. Besides, I have been scared of dogs in the past. I've been a target in two frightening chases by stray dogs while cycling down my street as a child. I was lucky to escape both times. Whereas, recently, your father and my mother have both been bitten by a stray dog. By the same one to be precise. The dog, who was a she and her name was Chandni.

Chandni, a stray dog, appeared on the street of my parental home in Krishna Nagar, the east of Delhi, about 12 years ago. But unlike the rest of my family, Chandni and I never got used to each other. The reason being—that I spent five years (2003-2008) in my Dental College hostel in Modinagar, a small town just on the outskirts of Delhi. During my hostel days, I would visit home every other weekend, and hence, Chandni always looked extremely terrifying to me. She was a stranger to me and, perhaps, the distrust was mutual. She was still there, waiting for me to scare me off with her loud bark, each time I stepped on the street. Chandni's skin was always covered with garbage dumped on the road that had been soaking in puddles. She had patches of all kinds of filth all over her body.

Every day, cars were parked on non-allocated spaces in the skinny streets of our colony. I often saw her sleeping under those cars or sometimes, on top of them. On some occasions, she found solace in unclogged drains that were waiting to be cemented and filled someday by someone from the local municipality.

I used to cautiously look for her before stepping out of my house and luckily if she wasn't in sight, I had to tip-toe on the street, just to make sure I don't wake her up. Anyway, soon enough, despite her repulsive appearance, Chandni became a familiar entity of the neighbourhood. Some generous people gave her leftovers from time to time. However, I'm not sure who had given her that name. She had begun to recognize the residents and scare off strangers on the street. Perhaps because of this mutual benefit, Chandni continued to survive on our street and was not kicked out of the neighbourhood. I called it our symbiosis.

Coming back to the present, despite going through a lot of hiccups with you both due to HBL, I am relearning some basics. There are 195 countries in the world today, according to one of your lessons. Undeterred by thousands of eye-opening stories and the exemplary efforts of icons from the little Peppa Pig to Taylor Swift to the great Dalai Lama, people still haven't been able to accept '*peace and harmony in all the world*'. This harsh reality extends to a racist mindset. Grudges can be attributed to a bitter historical event, a forged viral video showing animosity, a hoax call, sporadic episodes of social disturbances or resentment through propaganda that has been carried over generations. The reason doesn't matter, but some eccentric people have a zero-tolerance policy when it comes to offering their *turf*. As Meesha says when she's eating a bar of chocolate—*sharing is not caring*. Opportunities for xenophobes to vent their frustration arise now and then. One such outlet in the form of Coronavirus came this year, and China became both the victim and the culprit in the eyes of xenophobes. From London to Perth to Singapore, the anti-Chinese sentiment rose out of conjecture. And of course, to the rest of the ignorant people all around the world—all Asians look the same, so many (Chinese or not) had to face the music.

Personally, Coronavirus did brew up a storm of panic inside my usually not-so-hysterical mind. People who know me well, who have seen me at my best and my worst, who have spent a couple of decades or even a couple of days with me, would agree that I am often a clumsy and careless idiot. I have lost valuable treasures, missed irrevocable deadlines and have exposed myself to innumerous vulnerable situations. To make things worse, I have been a snob about escaping danger after such exposure, not as a cautionary tale, but as an expression of my adventurous persona. My constant need to do this and then brag about it to prove a point and feel honoured (in reality, *cocky*) has brought me a load of problems. I confess!

But Coronavirus shook my sense of complacency. To say the least, it landed accidentally like a missed blind spot in my life, smashed into it mercilessly and then haunted me with thoughts of crushing my family.

I suddenly found myself going that extra mile. I washed and disinfected my house again, and again, and again. I stopped buying chicken and seafood. This was when Coronavirus was still known by the bigoted name—*Wuhan virus,* after the Chinese city where it was first found to occur.

My initial jitters began when the figures started to rise. At one time, after mainland China, the next highest number of cases that were rapidly increasing daily, was in Singapore (barring the diamond princess cruise ship quarantined at Yokohama, Japan shore).

Then, Singapore raised its DORSCON—*Disease Outbreak Response System Condition*—alert level to *Orange,* which meant extra precautions with everyday life. Schools, offices, salons, restaurants were still open. Other countries undertook similar measures. These were meant to make people conscious and safe, but they also created public mayhem.

Whenever a new measure was announced, it brought with itself a whole new level of groundless hysteria. I've never had to stand in a queue for 45 minutes to pay at the supermarket. Seeing others panic made me panic and scramble all the more. When we couldn't get groceries, we fed you both oatmeal and eggs for all meals. We were flabbergasted by the sudden havoc. I bit my tongue and learnt my lesson that over-compensating for one family could leave others scarce.

'*Carpe. Carpe, Carpe diem. Seize the day, boys. Make your lives extraordinary.*' John Keating aka Robin Williams tells his students in the legendary movie—*Dead Poets Society*. But remember that he also said, 'There's a time for daring, and there's a time for caution. And a wise man understands which is called for.'

But alas, mindfulness and sensibility died a silent death. Homo Sapiens are strange. When you ask them to worry about stepping out, they party like their country has just won the World Cup—just as thousands of people all over the world repeatedly ignored lockdown and social distancing. People held parties and prayer meetings despite warnings. Some self-proclaimed superheroes not only hid their travel histories but also travelled across countries and cities using public transport. Yes, we didn't take the situation seriously for a long time.

And ironically but still strategically, when humans are asked to calm down, they cry at the top of their lungs. Some quarrel over toilet paper! Toilet paper was among the top-selling items the first weekend after Coronavirus reached Singapore and Australia. Next was instant noodles! Phew! Such a relief. Indians didn't have to deal with that particular problem. They were dependent on neither.

My new agenda now was to clean, clean and clean some more. I asked my family to treat their hands as sacred. To not let them touch anything unless they absolutely had to. Even if it is a pizza slice or a burger or a sandwich or even *roti*, they had to use cutlery. Period. It was unflattering, but it had to be done. Every frequently touched surface became red-flagged, including lift buttons, railings on escalators and even the bottom of all ladies' handbags. Well! The last one is a joke.

The struggles I speak of
Are just the hardest ones
For it sucks using a fork and a knife
To cut and eat that burger bun.

Just when the news of lockdown being lifted in China was being celebrated and admired all over, came a surprise. Lockdown was announced across many countries in Europe. Cases in Singapore were on the rise. This prompted concern from my family in India, a part of the world which was still unaffected at the time. We were asked to pack our bags and fly to India. I ignored their concerns, entrusting ourselves to the Singaporean government.

I reassured myself that it isn't what it looks like, and even if it is, it is always mind over matter! Frankly, it did help. I calmed down, and so did the commotion. Things streamlined and a *new normal* became more feasible. This was 'life under lockdown'.

Memes started showing up about the pros of a quarantined world. About making discoveries out of solitude! About treating it as a staycation and an opportunity to unwind! About learning new culinary skills! About getting healthier than you have ever been! But how many people took advantage of it as they should have? Probably not many.

But why didn't we? Or why couldn't we? It seems that humans are restless by nature. They need some action they can pursue daily, just so the day goes faster. And when the situation is something like the current one, we find a million things to modify and manipulate as per our interests. Just so that we have something to do and also get people to like us!

I finally started reading the long due Yuval Noah Harari's bestseller book *Sapiens*. It mentions a theory that suggests that we evolved to *Homo Sapiens* because of our ability to gossip. Gossiping proves that Homo sapiens are primarily social animals. But as you have learnt in school that *practice makes perfect*, we are all such champions at gossiping that it has evolved as our superpower. The misuse and misuse and then some more abuse of these superpowers had made us misinformed, self-righteous and highly ignorant.

I started getting a flood of forwarded messages, videos and news screenshots about Coronavirus facts and figures. Some said that China isn't declaring the actual casualties, while some presumed that the virus was made in a Chinese lab for war purposes and it leaked infecting their own. Frankenstein alert! In the world of sensationalism, this was exceptionally charismatic.

Some people thought outside the box and circulated random videos of Asian people in medical gowns carrying guns, captioning them as—*China is now shooting patients to arrest the spread.* These were horrifying and without a doubt fake. Someone even sent me a forwarded message that a *Chinese Aravind Adiga* (Yes, The Booker Prize winner) is capturing the truth and will write a letter to Modi *Ji*

(India's pre-eminent current Prime Minister) before he visits China to give the real picture. Preposterously creative, I must say.

BATS OR RATS OR CATS? What did China eat? One random person with a devilish brain thought of a way to use terror and spread it on the internet. It looked like a well-planned and brilliantly executed plan to manipulate people across the world emotionally.

Along with the countless scary videos, came a flood of blog posts and videos on social media platforms where many people from infected areas were and still are being treated as social outcasts globally. How people from Wuhan living in countries outside China, who didn't have the disease or even a recent travel history to China were being ostracized and labelled as the face of the disease. It was disgusting and unacceptable.

To bring up another theory from *Sapiens*. Harari says, *"Any large human-cooperation is rooted in common myths that exist only in people's collective imagination"*. For example, the way people across the globe, who have never met, still stay united over a Cricket match supporting their country. Or over tastebuds as in case of butter chicken or tiramisu fan-following. Or people keep following pop-culture blindly without being a loyal fan just to *keep up with the Kardashians*! Or the way doctors connect over the Hippocratic oath. Most recently, a majority of the ignorant pseudo-intellectuals of the world connected over the myth that China gave the world Coronavirus by eating bats. Remember the gossip theory from above? I rest my case!

The sources of these rumours had no integrity or credentials. The real message behind these Coronavirus wolf cries was—HIT LIKE, SHARE AND SUBSCRIBE!!! Unfortunately, and rather shamefully, not everyone questioned the authenticity and credibility of it all. I deleted such posts straightaway and asked our loved ones to do the same.

But this reminds me that such bias and hateful sentiment of human beings extends to how they treat other species too. Coming back to Chandni, she continued to live on our street. I, on the other hand, got married within a few months after getting back from the hostel and moved to Sydney with your father.

Chandni gave birth to 6 puppies after a couple of years. Coincidently, I was visiting Delhi at the time. Many people in the neighbourhood, myself included, thought that *it will be such a menace to have six grown-up street dogs who look so fierce just like their mother—Chandni*. But, maybe, just maybe, someone was listening, and all puppies died within a week. Regardless of whether I hoped for a sordid solution or not, I had tears in my eyes.

Seems Chandni was unbeaten. She got pregnant again after another year and gave birth to seven puppies this time. I got the news from my mother over the phone. History repeated itself, and all puppies died again, me hoping and praying for them to survive. All puppies were either malnourished or drowned in rainwater or just got smashed under cars. One day when my brother tried to drive, he inhaled an unpleasant smell and when he took the car to the mechanic, a dead new-born puppy, who had interestingly reached up there, perhaps to seek some warmth, was found in the car silencer. It was heartbreaking for everyone in the neighbourhood. Though nobody lifted a finger to rescue the newborns before the apocalypse, rather showed disgust and frowned when the time was right.

Notwithstanding, life had to go on. Even when Chandni was still fighting her apocalypse and even today when we are fighting ours. You must be thinking that I'm exaggerating as we didn't even get the disease. However, I called Coronavirus an apocalypse because of the collateral damage we faced. Apart from the extra cleaning, other smaller problems that came as a part of the deal were all associated with the lockdown. No friends or family get-togethers, no official meetings, no vacations, no brunch outings, no coffee chats, no gym (although this one I don't mind at all), no playgrounds and no schools!

Your friends would come running to our ground floor condominium balcony, hoping to play. They were always welcome to walk in and play before the Coronavirus circuit breaker was announced. Turning them away broke my heart. As if I were openly holding a big tray of candies on Halloween. But as soon as little kids dressed in spooky costumes arrived saying 'Trick or Treat', I said that I wouldn't give them any. In the five years of parenting, I had seen every meltdown there could be and thought nothing could break me now. I was counting on a misconception.

Social distancing became a law. But along with it came the unfortunate and unforeseen bigotry. Apart from anti-Chinese prejudice, there was and still is discrimination against many elements of the community. An illegal religious gathering in a country led to fanaticism against the entire religion. The poor and oppressed class of the society faced both the disease and the outcast sentiment due to their cooped up living situations. Children of doctors and nurses dealing with the pandemic were turned away from schools despite the mandatory 'stay at work' notices for their parents, long before the actual lockdown. People have been on the edge and hence gullible.

The untold plight of health care war heroes was terrible. But that's all a part of the job. And it's not even the worst part. Not even getting extensive skin reactions because of the crucial personal protective equipment (PPE). Not even having to wear diapers at work just so that they don't have to change the set of PPE during a shift due to limited numbers on hand. Not even the occupational hazard of being exposed to the disease every day, being mere mortals. What could be more troubling than not being able to go home and meet your family when you just want a warm hug from your family to get rid of all your woes? Heart-breaking!

Problems are problems. Some are small, some are bigger, and some are *ginormous*. Coronavirus has gifted fright, scarcity and isolation to humans. People who have seen their loved ones suffering, people who couldn't cremate their loved ones and people who couldn't even reach out to their loved ones in need have been the most affected. These have been the most gut-wrenching consequences of the disease. I'm not sure if there is enough empathy in the world to sublimate it all.

Lockdown has brought up a big debate to light. Is this nature's way of rebelling? Because from Jersey to Venice to Jalandhar, although people are locked down, nature is free-flowing. Birds are more audible, skies are bluer, and the air is purer.

Coming back to Chandni, my mother informed me that the animal again gave birth to 6 puppies in the second week of March 2020. She was very insecure this time. She became violent if anyone came closer than 2 metres to her babies. It had nothing to do with the social distancing norm for Coronavirus. She became hostile, probably after losing her babies in the past. She bit many people including maids, a child on a bicycle and a pizza delivery guy on our street. A couple of days later, she was found lifeless—dead like a street dog on the street. There were speculations that someone killed her on purpose to end the violence. It made me sick to my stomach. Couldn't the puppies have been born at another time when the world was not so morbid? In the Coronavirus situation, nobody would care for an enraged stray dog or worse, its orphaned puppies.

Everybody saw what happened, but as expected, apart from a few who poured leftover milk for the puppies in discarded plastic containers, nobody gave a damn.

Eventually, Delhi was also locked down, on the 24th of March. No traffic on the roads and lots of people inside their homes bored to death and trying to find a purpose in their quarantined lives. Coronavirus whirled up a frenzy in households. Everybody was panicking about sickness, lockdown, inevitable financial losses, social distancing, FOMO, grocery shopping, absence of the mighty domestic helpers, cancelled travels, no human contact, no dating, not even the old school two-wheeler stalking of girls that somehow satisfied the ever-deprived Delhi boy pheromones. Families sang to each other like Anna did to Elsa: "*We only have each other, what are we going to do*?" Brains began to swirl. Souls began to cringe. Hearts began to sink.

Then under these sentiments of hysteria mixed with a big load of anguish and melancholy, people of our colony came together for a cause—to care for six innocent lives. This paradoxical purpose came as a surprise when people saw six orphaned, helpless newborn puppies on the street. Within a couple of days, milk containers started accumulating around the little ones. Along with the abundance of milk, the puppies received plenty of warmth—both in the form of blankets and real human love from the donors. These people had found a new meaning during the lockdown. Playing with the puppies gave them unbound happiness. People were eager to get out of their houses, especially to be able to *make a difference*.

The six puppies are now grown up enough to run around the streets. They are treated like community pets who are being loved and cared for by all. The same people who were resentful towards their mother are being sanctimonious on social media platforms declaring how they are bringing up the babies of a dead stray dog. The little rascals were born with a silver spoon! Even though their mother died, they found their silver lining. Times of despair brought hope and brought life.

At this juncture, I visualize Pi Patel, the central character of Yann Martel's classic novel *Life of Pi*. The story, as we know, unfolds the struggles of a teenage boy trying to survive a shipwreck. The hapless Pi becomes stranded in the Pacific Ocean on a lifeboat with a ferocious tiger, named Richard Parker—much like Coronavirus. The tiger could devour the innocent boy instantly, but strangely enough, it succumbs to the love and affection shown by Pi and lets him live by his side. A bond between animals and human beings seems to have grown, making it possible for humans and animal species to coexist in harmony. Animals undoubtedly are the creation of nature, just as we are. We share the world with them: they deserve to live uninterrupted and to the fullest. The realization of this biocentric philosophy of life awakened my inner conscience. I vehemently decry the tendency of pseudo-intellectuals who put man at the centre of any story.

One of my friend's golden words of wisdom regarding the pandemic were: "Richa, we are crazy over the top extra worrying moms. We already wash our hands a hundred times a day and sanitize the table before sitting down to eat, buy fresh fully cooked food and most importantly, terrorize our kids over maintaining personal hygiene. I think we are already fighting against the virus. Just continue what you are already doing. I think we're good."

Today, Arjun and Meesha, I know that preventing my family from getting the disease is not in my hands. I know that everyone is doing their best. I know that everyone is a little bit scared. I know the only way to play safe is to stay home and wash hands. I know that it is what it is, but life has to go on. So, if after all this, someone still gets the disease, it sucks—but we shall overcome it. Be it the situation of Chandni or that of Coronavirus, does the how and why of all this matter? What matters is—if and when things will be back to the old normal. What matters amidst the unpredictability, hysteria and impatience is—whether we will backfire with *carpe diem* in our hearts or humbly give in and reciprocate.

From the challenging olden days,

Mamma
20th of April, 2020 (The year of Coronavirus)